CABO SUNSET

CABO
BOOK 3

ROBERT WISEHART

ROUGH
EDGES
PRESS

For Dana, mi corazon

CABO SUNSET

CHAPTER 1

I'D FORGOTTEN that I left my cell phone on vibrate. I had it in my pants pocket so when it vibrated with a call it was not an altogether unpleasant experience.

"Ethan Cruickshank."

"Ethan, you're not gonna believe this; it's Jeff LaForge."

Suddenly the experience became most unpleasant.

"Sorry to hear it," I said.

He sighed. "You haven't changed."

"Probably not," I said. "It's been a long time. What do you want?"

"I need to hire you," he said. "Can we meet?"

"Meet? We don't even live in the same country. You're in California and I'm in Mexico. Why don't you get somebody home grown?"

"I thought you knew," he said. "We've got a place in Cabo. We live here part time. Do a lot of business here, too."

Oh, hell, I thought. There goes paradise.

"Ethan, it's important. We may be in some trouble. Can we meet this afternoon? Please? We're not far away."

I liked "please," especially coming from LaForge.

"Lemme see if I can switch some things around," I said. "I'll call you back as soon as I can."

I was stalling for time. For all I had going on I could have met LaForge somewhere in Canada instead of in sunny Cabo San Lucas. I just wanted him to stew a little. Or a lot.

The other thing was that I couldn't stand him and he knew it. I wasn't sure that I wanted to meet with him at all. This was a man I once threatened to drown in a pot of hot chili. That made me wonder why he called me, of all people, which made our meeting irresistible. He knew it, too.

After ten minutes of doing nothing, I called back and agreed to meet him at a little restaurant in Cabo named Land's End.

LaForge was an old acquaintance from Southern California who made a vast pile of money and now apparently lived part of the year in Cabo San Lucas. The way it was rolling in the last I heard, he'd probably made billionaire by now. At one time, he was the owner and publisher of several newspapers and television stations west of the Rockies. He sold all of them to a national chain and got out before the business of print journalism started swirling around the drain. He started several dot.com endeavors, including an on-line publication named Focus that combined a little investigative journalism with the kind of snotty glorified gossip that seems to please people these days. Supposedly his digital empire was so successful that LaForge had gained a place up there with the Facebook and Amazon crowd.

Jeff LaForge was a good businessman, but an even better jerk. My dislike for him was visceral and struck deep the first time I laid eyes on him. We had our final run-in back when I lived in Southern California. My wife, Dina, had a public relations business and did some work for a couple of his companies so we ran into him socially from time to time. I watched him abuse underlings and suck up to anyone he needed. He was one of those people who could make "Good morning" sound like a sneer. He grated on me so much that even when he didn't say anything, I didn't like the way he didn't say it.

One night during a party at a beach house he owned in those days, LaForge was piqued because the chili that he bragged was his 'personal recipe" wasn't ready for the guests on time. With probably 50 people watching, he berated the young employee who was supposed to have it ready until she was in tears. I'd seen him pull that kind of power stunt a half-dozen times but for some reason that was the one that made me lose it. I trumped his over-reaction with one of my own. The next thing I knew I had him in a headlock as we advanced on the giant bubbling pot so I could bury his face in it. Once cooler heads separated us, he apologized for acting like a jackass, I apologized for threatening to drown him in his own recipe, and neither of us meant it. From that moment, he probably liked me even less than I liked him.

Dina never worked for him again. She said it was her choice. It probably cost her firm a quarter-of-a-million dollars over the years, though she never mentioned it.

All that rattled though my brain during the ten-minute drive from my house overlooking the spectacular beach just east of Cabo San Lucas to Land's End in the middle of downtown Cabo, a block from the marina, where I was shown to an outdoor table. Despite its location at the southern tip of the Baja Peninsula, for some reason the restaurant had a Caribbean theme, including reggae playing in the background. I didn't understand it but I didn't mind because the jerk chicken was the best I'd ever eaten.

LaForge was late, as usual. I remembered it as one of

his many irritating habits; his way of showing people how important he was. It was as if he never figured out that he really was important and didn't have to pound the point home by being a pain in the ass.

His handshake was firmer than necessary and he couldn't have been as happy to see me as he acted. Jeff LaForge was about six feet tall, a couple of inches shorter than I am, and looked like he weighed about the same, two hundred and ten pounds, thick through the torso with broad shoulders. I was pleased to see that his gut looked softer than I remembered. He wore a light blue short-sleeved linen shirt, white linen pants, and sandals. His graying hair was swept back from his forehead and just starting to thin, although he hid it well with a two hundred dollar haircut. His narrow face and dark skin showed his Cajun ancestry. A self-made man, he was born in a small town not far from New Orleans and had the accent to prove it. Cajuns don't talk like anyone else on earth. LaForge had smoothed his accent out over the years, but you could still hear traces of it, especially when he was angry or excited, when he sounded like he had a mouth full of marbles.

I had a can of Tecate on the table in front of me and my jerk chicken was on the way. LaForge glanced at my beer with a nicely developed sense of scorn and ordered an iced tea.

"Someone's threatening me," he said.

"Imagine that," I said. "Unless things have changed since we last saw each other, you'll be shocked to hear that a lot of people don't like you."

"That's cute," he said. "Do you enjoy watching me squirm?"

"Not as much as I hoped," I admitted. "So who's threatening you?"

He shook his head. "I don't know, but it's been going on for a while. To tell you the truth, I'm scared."

That got my attention. I knew LaForge well enough to know that he'd never admit he was scared unless he was genuinely petrified.

He explained that the Land Rover he kept in Cabo had been vandalized twice. The first time the windows were shattered. The second time all four of his tires were punctured. There were threatening letters, too, both in Cabo and at his permanent residence in Ventura, on the California coast about an hour's drive north of Los Angeles, along with more vandalism. And yesterday his Cabo housekeeper found a bullet in his mailbox, similar to one found in his Ventura mailbox a few days earlier.

"A bullet?" I raised my eyebrows. "That's a little dramatic. I saw that in a movie once."

"Yeah, 'The Insider', the one with Russell Crowe and Al Pacino," he said. "I thought of that, too."

"What caliber was it?" I asked.

He shook his head. "I don't know anything about that kind of stuff. What does that have to do with it anyway? I mean, should I feel better if it's smaller, or something?"

I took a small sip of my beer. It was too early to have another one and I wanted it to last.

"So why do you need me?" I asked. "The police in both places are pretty good at this kind of thing. I know the chief here. He's as good as you'll find anywhere."

My jerk chicken arrived and I dug in while Bob Marley sang, 'No Woman, No Cry' in the background. I liked Jimmy Buffet better but Marley would do. LaForge passed the time by taking a drink of his iced tea and dabbing at his lips with a paper napkin.

"First off, it's happening here *and* back home," he said. "So somebody's pretty damn serious. I did call the police but I want more than that. I don't know anything about the Cabo police but you know as well as I do that the cops back home don't exactly love me."

There was a time when LaForge was controversial. Maybe he still was. I hadn't paid attention for a long time. Years ago, one of his newspapers ran an investigative series on the police department in Ventura. Among other things, it found that some old-timers were taking payoffs, mostly nickel and dime stuff. At the same time, some of the younger cops had a habit of using about ten times the necessary force in certain arrests, most of which seemed to involve anybody who wasn't white. It had happened years earlier and the police department dealt with it quietly and internally. The veterans were forced into early retirement and the younger guys were let go because they didn't have the "temperament" for police work.

Nobody outside the department knew what happened until LaForge got a tip and turned two good reporters loose on it for a couple of months. As is the case with so much journalism, everything printed was accurate but not necessarily the truth. The stories went national and gave the impression that the whole department was rotten and the cops were running wild. It wasn't and they weren't, but none of that mattered.

The chief, a good man who'd brought the department out of the dark ages but probably stayed too long on the job, wound up retiring earlier than he wanted to, his reputation shot to hell. He'd spend the rest of his life playing a lot of golf. He liked golf, but probably not that much.

"To tell you the truth, if those guys had anything to work with I think they'd bust their butts on this," I said. "But it wouldn't be for any great love of you. It'd be their way of saying, 'Up yours, LaForge.'"

Judging by his skeptical look, LaForge didn't buy it. I

wasn't surprised. Assuming that the world had it in for him added to his already considerable self esteem. A man with powerful enemies must be a powerful man.

"So why me?" I asked. "There are a lot of PIs around."

"Not with your background," LaForge said. "You know what's going on up there and you know what's going on down here."

I wasn't sure that I knew what was going on anywhere, but I *was* sure that he didn't like asking for my help. I didn't know how I felt about giving it either. LaForge covered the awkward moment by draining the last of his ice tea.

His eyes widened when I told him my rate.

"You're more expensive than you used to be," he said.

"You can afford it."

"You know, I never understood why you left the country, much less moved here," he said.

"You don't have to understand," I said. "I do."

CHAPTER 2

LaForge said he had to go back to California for a few days, but he'd keep in touch. In the meantime, I wanted to get a feel for where he lived in Cabo. I'd probably have to visit his place in California and contact the police there, too. I'd been there a couple of times, but that was years ago.

But first I wanted to talk to Valencia, chief of the Cabo San Lucas police department.

I called, he was in, and I drove over from the restaurant. It took maybe five minutes.

The Cabo police department is located in a cinder block building on an unpaved street well out of sight from where tourists are wont to dwell. Tourism is Cabo's business, virtually its only business, and the police presence is deliberately low key. Visitors are aware of it, but it isn't threatening. The drug-related crime that plagues so much of Mexico is absent here because it's far away from the drug routes to the United States and no cartels fight over the turf. Like anyplace that caters to tourists, Cabo has other crime problems, but usually not big ones, thanks, in large part, to Valencia, whose background included training at the FBI Academy in Quantico and a stint with Interpol in Geneva.

After a more than awkward meeting a few years ago – Valencia threatened to throw me in jail – we'd become friends, sort of. He was a good cop, one of the best I've ever known, and took his job seriously.

As I stepped through the door of the Cabo *policia*, it occurred to me that Valencia might not be happy to see my smiling face on official business. Since moving to Cabo, I'd been involved in two of the biggest and messiest local crimes in years. He might not be thrilled to learn that I'd taken another case in his town.

The desk cop, a fat old guy who looked like a Mexican Buddha with a walrus mustache, casually waved me through to Valencia's office, where most of the space was taken up by an institutional metal desk, an institutional metal filing cabinet, and two institutional visitor's chairs, along with a view of the institutional parking lot out back. One wall featured a large street map of Cabo San Lucas with green pins scattered over it. I'd never bothered to ask what the pins meant.

Valencia was on the telephone and waved me to one of the chairs. As usual, there was a cup of coffee on the desk in front of him. If I drank as much coffee as he did, I'd have the shakes all day long.

He put the telephone down and leaned back in his chair, neat and slim as ever in his blue uniform, black mustache and well barbered dark hair. No matter the circumstances, he seemed to bring a kind of precise control to everything he did. Only an occasional formality of phrasing revealed that English was not his native language.

"I know why you are here," he said.

"Jeff LaForge," I said.

"Yes, LaForge," he said. "He said that he would contact you. By the way, I don't like him."

"Not many do." I told Valencia everything that LaForge told me. "Now, what can *you* tell me?"

"Not much more than what he told you. What he says happened seems to have happened."

"What are you doing?"

"We are looking into it, but there isn't much to see. He lives in a gated community called The Palms, built around a Greg Norman-designed golf course. Anyone who gained access probably came in from the beach, which would be easy to do. Security is not tight. I have a patrol go past his home twice a day, both on the street and on the water. He also has a large business facility here, which is where he spends most of his time when he is in the area. As you know, we are not a large department and we are stretched already. Considering that he is a man of means, I suggested that he hire extra security, which, I suppose, is you."

"I'm an investigator, not security, and I'm only one guy. Go back a minute. You said he had a large facility here. I didn't know that. What kind of facility and where? How long has it been here?"

Valencia took a swallow of coffee, got up, took two steps to a coffee maker on top of the filing cabinet, poured another cup, and returned to his chair.

"I am not surprised that you don't know, although I am surprised that he didn't tell you. What's the word … outsourcing? People work here for a fraction of what they earn in the United States. LaForge kept it low key, probably to avoid bad public relations at home, where outsourcing is not a welcome concept these days. It's a building of several hundred thousand square feet, which is used for storage, distribution, international communication, taking orders, and things such as that. There are rumors that he has plans to build elsewhere in Mexico, perhaps two other such facilities, which means that, at the moment, he is much favored by the government."

Valencia got up again, walked around from behind his desk and pointed to a spot on the Cabo map.

"It is located here," he said.

Valencia's finger was pointed at the north part of town, a mix of a few strip malls used by the locals and light and heavy industry where tourists might go only if they were lost.

It was interesting that LaForge didn't mention it. I wondered why.

"What is it for?" I asked. "What's the business?"

"I understand that it is a rival of Amazon, only without the books, which he believes eat up too much time, space, and effort, without sufficient profit."

I digested that for a moment. It sounded like LaForge was doing even better than I thought.

"Do you know we have a history?" I asked.

"He did say something about it, but gave no details. Who he hired and what he hired them to do is his affair as long as no laws are broken, which, now that you're involved, will most likely happened right and left."

"You're a funny man, for a police chief," I said, not entirely sure that he was kidding. "Were you able to trace the bullet?"

"From somewhere in China," he said.

"China?" I repeated. "In other words, it's not traceable."

"It happens quite a bit," Valencia explained. "That part of the world has become a major source of arms of all kinds."

I digested that bit of useless information.

"Anything else?"

Valencia nodded. "I talked to a detective in California." He pulled a file out of a desk drawer and rummaged though it. "His name is Tom Hauser and he confirmed what LaForge said about what happened there."

"Any conclusions?"

Valencia nodded again. "We agreed on one possibility, but it is just a possibility."

When Valencia smirked I knew what was coming.

"He thinks he's quite a stud, doesn't he?" I said. "It gets him in trouble sometimes, or at least it used to."

"As I understand it, his history is that if it has a heartbeat, he's after it; tall, short, old, young, ugly, beautiful. He reminded me of the former governor of California … Schwarzenegger, or your President Clinton. Not very a discriminating man. He thinks that he is *materia caliente*."

My Spanish was up to the task. "Hot stuff?" I grinned. "Yeah, that's Jeff. So you think maybe a pissed off husband or a boyfriend might be behind this?"

Valencia shrugged. "I don't know. But that does seem to be a constant thread in his life. What's interesting is that the threats and vandalism happened both in Southern California and here, which implies a high degree of seriousness, more than one person, or perhaps both."

"Yeah," I sighed. "Let the fun begin."

CHAPTER 3

Now I had to have a talk to Abby LaForge. Considering that, among other things, I was going to ask her about her husband's infidelities, I wasn't looking forward to it.

Before she married Jeff, Abby was one of the best feature writers in the business. Her specialty was the long, gossipy and slightly bitchy profile. She didn't write often, but every story was an event, the kind of thing that people talked about for days afterward.

When LaForge showed up in her life you could see her go on the prowl, although he wasn't hard to stalk. He was seeing someone else, but Abby blew past her as if she didn't exist. At first they tried to hide their relationship, but after a while it didn't matter because everybody knew what was going on. They finally got married in a quickie ceremony in Las Vegas. Abby continued working for a while but her heart wasn't in it. Being married to the top man was a little awkward, even for her.

I had no idea what she was doing now other than being Jeff's wife, but I'd find out soon enough.

Their house was in the corridor about halfway between Cabo San Lucas and San Jose Del Cabo, the two towns at the tip of the Baja Peninsula that make up Los

Cabos, one of the world's favorite playgrounds. Mine was in the corridor, too, but I lived much closer to Cabo San Lucas. More modestly, too.

I showed my ID and the guard at the gate pulled up the barrier and let me in. Not the best security I've ever seen, but at least it was something. I drove about a half mile with the golf course on my right, turned left along a road that paralleled the beach, and then turned right into the driveway. Another fifty yards and I came to the house. The development was set up so that no residence could be seen from any other residence, with the plush golf course winding among the homes. Cabo had become a golf Mecca over the last few years and this development was one example. All the big designers had courses here, including Nicklaus, Weiskopf, Norman, and others. Golf threatened to replace fishing as the area's main attraction. The LaForge house was white stucco and seemed to naturally fit into the rolling landscape in a very expensive way; Frank Lloyd Wright by way of Cabo San Lucas. Although I couldn't see it, I knew that the beach was at the back of the house. In Cabo, you can always feel the ocean because it's never far away.

The driveway ended in a circle in front of the house. There were two levels, with a deep porch running across the width of the first and a balcony along the second. Seen from the front, they looked like they probably went all the way around the house.

I pressed the doorbell and heard the three-tone chimes inside. A woman in a white uniform dress and black apron answered the door.

"*Senor* Crackshock?" she asked.

I decided that was close enough and nodded, assuming that the gate guard called ahead to tell Abby I'd arrived.

"The *senora* is at the swimming pool," she said. "She said you should go back. I will escort you."

The house was much wider than it was deep from front to back, the better to catch the sea breeze all though the house. I followed the woman though a living room where a thick red-patterned rug was laid over white tile, through another open room with a high ceiling that made only a fleeting impression, and stepped out onto a tiled patio set high above the ocean with the kind of view that only money can buy. The arch, the quintessential symbol of Cabo San Lucas, was off at a distance to the right. The sky was a deep tropical blue while the ocean, a meeting of the Pacific and the Gulf of California, looked like it belonged on a postcard, with just enough wave action to make is picturesque. The infinity pool had a Jacuzzi on the right and a waterfall on the left, with a blue-and-white striped cabana overlooking the beach on the other side of the pool from the house.

As nice as the view was, I was only vaguely aware of it because I was greeted by an even more spectacular sight – Abby LaForge in a bikini stretched out on a chaise lounge.

Well, only half of a bikini. She didn't have her top on.

As a trained detective attuned to detail and nuance, I could tell she did that a lot because her tan was all over, as least all over the parts I could see. Somehow a few other details registered, too. Her naturally blonde hair was cut mid-length and blue eyes sparkling with sass and intelligence highlighted her face. In her mid-thirties, she had the goods and she knew it. Her whole attitude toward men seemed to say, "Take your best shot, Bozo. We both know it won't be good enough but it might be amusing if you try." All her life, heads turned wherever she walked by, thanks to her combination of looks, smarts

and attitude. Right now my head was practically spin-
ning like something out of "The Exorcist."

We were never close friends, but she rose from the
chaise lounge, shrugged into a light terry cloth robe that
didn't quite close, and hugged me as if we were. The hug
was a combination of uncomfortable and absolutely
terrific. I wanted to do it again and get the hell out all at
the same time.

Abby asked if I wanted something to drink. I said that
a soft drink or iced tea would be fine. I didn't really want
anything, but sometimes the ceremony of it helps break
the ice, although given her state of undress there wasn't
much ice to break. If nothing else, I figured the delay
might help me settle down. She talked into an intercom
set up by the pool. The same woman who answered the
door shortly appeared carrying a tray with a Coke for me
and an Arnold Palmer for Abby, which she put on a glass
table.

"Ethan, stop looking so uncomfortable," she laughed,
knowing that her robe wasn't fully cinched in the front.
"And please, sit down."

I sat in a chair with blue-and white-striped cushions
beside the table. Abby sat on the edge of a matching love
seat that faced my chair at right angles so that our feet
were almost touching. Her back was to the swimming
pool.

And so we stared at each other, each of us waiting for
the other to say something.

"You don't look like somebody who's in fear for their
life," I said.

She responded with a sunbeam of a smile.

"No, I guess I'm not, though maybe I should be. For
some reason, it doesn't seem real to me. I know Jeff is
pretty rattled, though."

We went over the vandalism, the bullets, the threatening notes, why her husband hired me, and everything else I could think of. She said she hadn't heard a thing when the car was torn up. Their bedroom was on the second floor overlooking the pool in back, so she wasn't in a good position to hear anything in front of the house, where Jeff parked his car when it was vandalized, although I'd noticed a garage on one side of the house. As far as she knew, nothing unusual had happened when her husband was away, which was frequently. Whoever did it must have known he was in Cabo at the time, which probably meant that they were watching.

"I'm an awfully sound sleeper." She tossed her head to get an imaginary lock of hair out of her face. "Most of the time the house could come down around me and I probably wouldn't hear it."

"You don't go with him when he travels back and forth?"

"Not usually. To tell you the truth, I like it here a lot more than I thought I would."

I asked if she knew about any other threats.

"A few goofy crank calls and letters over the years," she said. "Jeff probably mentioned them. It's the usual stuff for somebody with a high profile. But this time Jeff thinks it's different. There's more of it and I guess it just feels different somehow."

There was another awkward pause while we stared at each other.

"How long has it been since Dina died, Ethan? A year or so?"

"One year, two months, nineteen days," I said.

My wife, my girl, and the love of my life died of an embolism while she was scuba diving in the Gulf of California. She'd taken up diving shortly after we moved to Cabo and loved it. She was an expert, too. There was no rhyme or reason to her death. It just happened.

The wound inside me was still there and always would be. In one way, I wanted it to be there for the rest of my life. But in another, I knew that I needed to move on, or at least try. The problem was that I didn't know how. I didn't really want to.

"How are you doing?" Abby asked.

"Okay, I guess. About how you'd expect."

I don't know why I kept talking, but I did.

"Hell, Abby, I don't even know what that means. I live. I do things. I function in the world. I can even laugh. But it's like I'm not all there. Maybe I'll never be all there. Sometimes, a lot, really, I forget and turn to say something to her just so I can hear her laugh."

After a moment, Abby rose to her feet. She untied the robe and stepped out of it. When she reached out to take my hand I felt the way someone must feel under hypnosis. I knew what was going on, but it was as if I didn't have a will of my own.

With my hand in hers, she led me into the blue and white cabana, which was open on the ocean side to catch the breeze and capture the view. There was nothing between us and the ocean but a steep down slope leading to a hundred yards of sand. My eyes never left her naked and bronzed back as we entered the cabana.

Our love-making was ferocious. We went after each other like two animals just let out of a cage as we rolled back and forth across the cushioned cabana floor. By the time we finished, we were covered in perspiration.

After a few minutes in each others' arms, Abby took my hand again and led me out of the cabana, down the pool steps, and into the water. It was cool and refreshing and wonderful with her body clinging to mine.

After a few minutes to cool off, we got out of the pool, returned to the cabana and toweled each other off, which inevitably led to more lovemaking, this time slower and gentler than before.

When we finished, both of us satiated, Abby called and asked the housekeeper, whose name was Imelda, to bring a bottle of white wine and two glasses out to the pool, "assuming wine is okay with you," she whispered, squeezing my hand.

"It's fine," I said, which may have been the understatement of the year. Battery acid would have been okay with me.

Imelda left the wine and glasses in a bucket on a table by the pool without disturbing our privacy. Stark naked, Abby left the cabana to get it and brought it back inside, where she poured for both of us before we resumed our position holding each other, the ocean breeze caressing our bodies much in the same way we had caressed each other.

"Are you okay," she whispered in my ear.

"Yeah, I am," I replied, whispering just as she did. "There's some part of me that says I shouldn't be, but I really am."

I rose on one elbow.

"Abby, what the hell just happened?"

She giggled. "That's pretty obvious, isn't it?"

I grinned. "You know what I mean."

Abby hesitated before answering. She didn't do that often.

"I think I wanted to make love to you for a long time, going back to before I met Jeff and before you got together with Dina."

"You know, I felt the same way about you in those days," I said.

Abby looked at me with surprise all over her face.

"Why didn't you *do* something?"

I took another moment to put my thoughts together.

"Pride, I guess. You already had too many guys hanging around you with their tongues out and their tails wagging. I didn't want to join the parade."

"Christ! If I'd only known ..."

"Then you met Jeff and you know how we always rubbed each other the wrong way. Then our lives went their separate ways and that was that ... until now."

"It's strange how it's come full circle, isn't it?"

"Well, maybe not full circle," I said. "Things aren't exactly the same as they were back then, are they?"

Her fingers gently ran along the side of my face.

"Except for right now. We can hold the moment for as long as we can."

CHAPTER 4

WE SPENT the night in the cabana. Without saying anything, both of us knew that once I left it would be as if nothing happened. Wonderful as it was, and as healing as it felt for me, there were so many things wrong with it that it would not - it could not - be repeated.

But before I left, I had to do what I'd come to do.

Characteristically, Abby took it head on.

"Ethan, do you want to know why you're really here?"

I had a pretty good idea. But, with her head cocked back and her chin tilted up, it was clear that I was being challenged so I went along with it.

"Why don't you enlighten me?"

"You're here because you want to know if Jeff is fucking anybody but me. And you want to know about anyone he fucked before me in case some husband or boyfriend holds a grudge. Is that about right?"

If it was meant to be shocking, it failed. For one thing, it was pure Abby. She always enjoyed the preemptive strike. There was something else going on, too. It was as if she was trying to prove something, if not to me then to herself.

"I wouldn't put it exactly that way," I said. "But I guess that's close enough."

And so, with both of us naked in paradise, we had a nice little chat about her husband's love life. It was as strange a conversation as I've had in a while. Abby seemed to collect the names the way other people collect stamps or baseball cards.

Being the dutiful investigator, I rustled though my clothes, found my notebook, and wrote down the names, dates and places. Abby seemed to know them all, or at least most of them, although I'd bet some exaggeration was involved, either on her part or, more likely, on his. She was uncomfortably specific, too. I wondered how she knew. Was LaForge bragging when he told her? Or was he trying to come clean about his past? One motive might be admirable, if a trifle weird. I was pretty sure the other one was repulsive.

"Of course, I'm not exactly Snow White either." She cocked her head again in that defiant way. "I've always been honest about liking men."

"After what happened here, I think I get it."

"You're different, Ethan. What happened was good for both of us. But it's important for me that you know I'm not my reputation. Some people think that every time I talk to a man I must be screwing him. The funny thing is I've always been pretty selective, but I always got along with men better than women anyway. Most of the women I know resent me and I don't blame them. I've always been able to pretty much do what I wanted on my own terms."

"Jealousy?" I asked.

"Something like that," she said.

Coming from someone else, it would have been arrogance, but Abby made it seem like a simple declaration of fact.

I flipped my notebook closed.

"I do have one more question, but it has nothing to do with the investigation. Does Jeff know that Dina died? I'm just curious. You obviously knew, but if he did he didn't mention it."

Abby shook her head. "I don't know, Ethan. We never talked about it. Anyway, you know how he is. If it doesn't concern him then he doesn't care."

"How did you know?"

"I'm not sure. Somebody told me, I guess. But I don't remember who. Pretty much everybody back home knows. You know how it is, word gets around."

It was already mid-morning. I'd stayed too long. We dressed, left the cabana, and started toward the house. On the way, Abby grabbed my arm, pressing her excellent chest against it as we walked. As we faced each other at the front door outside of the house, if we'd put our arms up, we could have slow danced.

"Nice ride," she said, eyeballing the Mustang for the first time.

"Yeah," I agreed, "it is."

I drive a '65 Mustang convertible. It was Arcadian blue with white leather interior and 289 cubic inch engine. Every time I drove it I felt like I was the coolest thing going.

After walking around the Mustang and admiring it in a hands-on way I'd grown quite familiar with overnight, she said, "I know Jeff's your client, but you'll keep me *informed*, won't you?"

"Of course, I will. I might even have to come around again. Is that okay?"

"I'd be disappointed if you didn't," she said.

"Abby, I suppose there *is* one more question," I said.

"So ask."

"What the hell are you doing with a jerk like Jeff?"

A quiet smile and a little shrug, as if to indicate that she didn't understand it either.

"I guess, in my way, I love him. And, in his way, he loves me."

CHAPTER 5

I DROVE HOME and put in serious time on the computer and working the telephone, learning everything I could about Jeff LaForge.

I jumped right into more work because I was getting paid for it and because I had nothing else to do and no one to talk to. Our beloved dog, a hundred-pound brown and black beast named Brewster, died three months after Dina's death. The vet said otherwise, but I knew that he grieved himself to death. There were times when I wanted to join him. Especially at night, I never knew a house could be so lonely.

Although I learned a lot, nothing unusual, or at least pertinent to what I was supposed to be doing, jumped out at me in my research. Mostly it confirmed what I already knew or suspected. LaForge was ridiculously rich. While he reported to a board of directors, there were two levels of stock and he owned a majority of the stock that controlled the complex series of inter-locking companies he created, which meant that he dominated the board he was supposed to report to. He served on a half-dozen other boards of directors, all of them national, or international, companies. He'd been married three times, and he'd lived in five states. He owned a house in California, a house in Cabo, and a condo in Aspen. He had one child, a son by a previous marriage who was enrolled at the University of Florida. He graduated *magna cum laude* from the University of Mississippi. One ex-wife lived in Chicago and the other lived in Dallas. Both had remarried and there seemed to be no residue hostility, although I marked it as something to be checked out. He belonged to several professional state, national, and world-wide organizations and was an officer in three of them. There were no judgments, liens or lawsuits filed by or against him, which was remarkable for a man in his position. He gave twenty to twenty five speeches a year and seemed to revel in his high profile. He worked out regularly, but had never played organized sports. In addition to Focus, which seemed to combine the characteristics of the National Enquirer with some serious reporting, as Valencia said, he had become a serious rival to Amazon, only without the books, which was my favorite part of Amazon. After several years of aggressive acquisition, he owned part or all of several of the companies that made what he sold. The width and breadth of his holdings was impressive, to say the least.

What struck me most was how LaForge was constantly on the move. He was the kind of person whose life involved squeezing ten pounds of mud into a five-pound bag on a daily basis.

I also found out why I missed the ground breaking of his facility in Cabo San Lucas. It happened at about the same time that Dina died, which was at about the same time he bought a residence here. I'd missed a lot during that period. It was like a giant hole in my life.

My next stop was California. I had a flight in the morning.

They say that the best way to combat loneliness was to stay busy. At least that's what they told me. But I'd run out of things to do. It was a long night. I sat outside, listened to the surf pound, and drank myself to sleep. I did that too often these days.

CHAPTER 6

THE FLIGHT NORTH WAS A BREEZE. Cabo's constantly expanding airport was easy to handle. The Los Angeles airport and the drive north was not. What should take less than ninety minutes took three hours. Nothing had changed in Southern California.

I opted for a professional look – navy blue blazer with brass buttons, light gray slacks, white long-sleeved shirt, a red and blue striped tie, and black loafers. Dashing, yet subdued.

The police department was in an imposing brick building next to the new jail. By some quirk of architecture, the police department looked more intimidating than the jail. I wondered if they did that on purpose. I parked in one of the visitor's spots at the side of the building, walked through the big double glass doors and told the desk man that I had an appointment to see Detective Hauser.

The desk man looked like a man who rode a desk all day long. His belly did a nice job of hiding his belt buckle. He picked up a telephone, punched in an extension, and growled, "You've got a visitor."

About thirty seconds later, Hauser emerged from a

door behind the desk. He couldn't have been more than five nine and seemed almost as wide. The man was a serious weightlifter. His neck was wider than his head. It looked like his collar might burst open any second and send the button flying across the room. The sleeves on his white shirt were rolled up to reveal forearms like bowling pins. Shaking his hand was like grabbing a chunk of pig iron. He had neatly combed brown hair and a thick brown mustache.

"C'mon back," he said.

It was still early and the room was uncharacteristically quiet. There were two other detectives at their desks. Both of them were on the telephone. Hauser settled into his chair with a chorus of metallic squeaks. I took the straight-back chair next to his desk.

"Where do you work out?" I asked.

"In my garage mostly," he said. "I did some amateur lifting when I was younger and just stayed with it. It's like jogging. If I go a couple of days without I miss it."

"Yeah, I can see that," I said.

Hauser grinned. "With short arms and a twenty-three inch neck, it's kinda hard to find clothes that fit, though."

He reached into a lower desk drawer and brought out a white coffee mug.

"Coffee?" he asked.

"No thanks," I said. "I've had plenty."

"I'll be back in a sec."

He got up and walked down the aisle between two rows of gray metal desks to a coffee maker on a table against the back wall, where he poured a cup of coffee with two sugars and a dash of cream. His huge arms seemed awkward making such small motions.

He returned to his desk, took a sip and grimaced.

"Every time I think I can't get worse, it does."

Hauser opened a manila file folder on his desk. Other

than the telephone, the only other thing on the desk was a plastic cube with photographs on the sides. Every picture was of the same person, a cute girl with lots of blonde hair who looked about fifteen years old. One photo showed her playing basketball. In another one she was outside by a stream reading a book. A third was a formal studio portrait. I couldn't see the fourth side of the cube. Unless the mother was there, and I didn't think she was, I'd bet that Tom Hauser was the divorced or widowed father of a terrific-looking teenage daughter.

"Okay, here's what we've got," he said. "Several times in less than a month the very wealthy Jeff LaForge was either threatened or had his property vandalized. The letters, if that's what you want to call 'em, were on lined notebook paper. They were written, not typed. One twenty two caliber bullet was found in his mailbox. There were no prints. Nobody saw or heard anything. There are no suspects and the investigation is ongoing. LaForge doesn't have a clue as to who it might be. At this point, neither do we."

"Let me guess," I said. "You tried to trace the bullet and it's from China, which means it's untraceable. "

"Yeah," he said. "Just like down in Cabo."

"What are you doing?" I asked.

"We run patrols by his house more often than we normally would, normally being not at all," he said. "We don't have many calls in his neighborhood. An un-mowed lawn is considered a reign of terror."

I asked if I could have copies of the letters and the police report.

"LaForge already asked us to cooperate with you," Hauser said.

"Is this the first time he's been threatened?"

Jeff and Abby already answered that question, but I wanted to see if they told the police the same thing.

"It's the first time he reported it," Hauser said. "According to LaForge, there've been a few crank calls and letters over the years, but nothing that seemed serious and nothing this close together. Just the kind of crap every public figure has to put up with, especially someone who's a well-known trillionaire."

"That it?" I asked.

Hauser hesitated. "There is one other thing."

"What's that?"

"He's a hound, or he was anyway."

"Yeah," I said, "I know."

"An angry husband or boyfriend, maybe?" Hauser said.

"Maybe," I replied. "The Cabo cops think that might be the best bet."

"Cabo cops any good?"

"The chief is."

It was time to clear something up.

"I know LaForge asked you to cooperate with me, but is that gonna be a problem?" I asked.

"Probably not," he said. "I checked you out. You're okay or you wouldn't be seeing my happy, cooperative self. We'd just stall you 'till the end of time. You left Southern California under circumstances best described as mysterious, but you're clean. You've got friends in important places, too. You know as well as I do that a private cop can give this thing more attention than we can. You know how it is. Assuming nothing else happens, the more time passes the more it slides down the list. LaForge seemed shocked that we have one or two other things to do."

By friends in important places, Hauser probably meant Harvey Grant, U. S. Senator from California. Before he was elected and before I moved to Cabo, his baby was kidnapped and I got involved in the case. It didn't turn out well but Grant didn't hold it against me.

Hauser drained the last of his coffee. "Besides, if I did mind, would it matter?"

"Nope," I said. "But it might make it harder."

He gave me a level stare. "You *will* let us know if you turn up something?"

"Sure." I handed him my card. "You'll do the same?"

"Oh, hell yes." He opened the desk's middle drawer and put the card on the tray inside. "What else do I have to do?"

"Detective Hauser, do I sense sarcasm?" I asked.

"Nothing gets by you, does it?" he said.

"There is one more thing," I said. "I assume you're checking the cop angle on LaForge. I doubt that there's anything to it, but it's gotta be looked at and it'd be a lot easier for you than for me."

"Yeah, I'm looking at it, but I don't think it'll amount to anything either. If somebody in the department wanted to hassle LaForge they'd have done a long time ago. Besides, there are better and less stupid ways to do it. Just the same, I'm concentrating on the guys who were forced out. There were some screws loose in that group, guys who never should have been hired in the first place. I'll let you know if I find anything but I doubt that I will."

We both stood up to shake hands.

"By the way, I'm sorry about your wife," he said.

Reacting to my frown, he added, "It came up when I checked you out. Didn't mean to offend."

"Don't worry about it," I said. "You didn't. And thanks."

From the police station, I drove my rented Kia across town to the LaForge headquarters while I listened to Terry Gross on NPR's "Fresh Air." She was interviewing the director of a film I hadn't seen yet. The more they talked about it the more I didn't want to see it.

The building took up about half a block in an office park area with employee parking on both sides. I checked in with the guard at the desk just inside the entrance. His name was Bernie and he'd been the "security chief" for as long as anyone could remember. By most estimates, he was about four thousand years old. He came on like a combination of Wild Bill Hickok and the most irritating bureaucrat you've ever met. Someone could steal his chair out from under him and old Bernie probably wouldn't notice, but let someone commit a dastardly parking violation in the lot and he was on them like the wrath of a very old and wizened God.

When I signed in he handed me a clip-on badge that said "VISITOR" in bold black letters. I slipped it in my pocket.

"You're supposed to clip that on your lapel," Bernie protested.

"Yeah, I know," I said. "I must be the anti-Christ."

I took the escalator to the second floor, signed in with the receptionist, and walked across a big room full of badly dressed youngish workers doing whatever the hell they were doing with their faces buried in computer screens to LaForge's glass-enclosed office in the back.

LaForge was standing behind his desk with his iphone to his ear. The office walls were covered with photographs of LaForge with an array of movers and shakers from Presidents and kings to celebrities and Senators, a wonderful monument to himself. He saw me through the glass and waved me in. He was in his shirt-sleeves, a white shirt with thin light gray lines. His tie was a patterned dark gray. The suspenders were black. The pants were charcoal. He looked swell.

"Okay," he said, bending over to scribble something as he talked. "I'll see you then."

He put the iphone on his desk and handed me a bright blue folder.

"Here's a list of projects we're working on at Focus, plus everything major we've done for the last couple of years," he said. "Who knows, maybe there's something there that might help you."

He buttoned his shirt collar and pulled his tie up tight. He walked out from behind his desk, reached in back of the door to his office, pulled a suit jacket off of its hanger and shrugged into it.

"I've gotta go to a meeting," he said. "I'm late already. Mort'll go over all that stuff with you and anything else you need. Whatever you want. Call me later."

He moved toward the door but I was in his way. He stopped, not sure what to do.

"So tell me, Jeff, how's your love life?" I asked.

"What?" His voice was somewhere between irritation and surprise.

"Any angry boyfriends or husbands out there who might have something to do with what's going on?" I asked.

He started to say something but stopped when I raised my hand.

"Don't tell me it's none of my business," I said. "Even you know better than that. Nothing's off limits. That's the way it has to be."

He seemed to deflate a little, but it didn't last long.

"Hang on." He stepped around me, shut the office door, and turned to face me again.

"Look, Ethan, I know how my past looks and I'm not proud of it. But there hasn't been anyone other than Abby since we got married. All that's over for me. It's been that way for a long time."

"Even if you're telling the truth that doesn't mean it's over for somebody else," I said, knowing that, if anything, he probably was very proud of it. "People carry grudges. Maybe it's payback time."

In the silence that followed, I had the impression that LaForge was thinking more about how to say something than what to say.

"Ethan, I swear that whatever's going on has nothing do with any of that," he said. "There are no jealous husbands or boyfriends crazed with anger lurking around somewhere. I can honestly say that none of my affairs ended badly. They ran their course and then they were over. Like I said, all that's way in the past anyway. Why would somebody wait this long? Now I'd appreciate it if you'd get out of my way. I've *got* to go."

"One other thing," I said. "Why didn't you tell me you had a big facility in Cabo?"

This time he was genuinely surprised.

"I thought you knew. What kind of private detective are you that you didn't know that I was one of the largest employers down there?"

Good old Jeff, I thought. Always assumes that he's the center of the universe.

"Some details get by even me. Why Cabo? Why not the usual? You know, India, China, or someplace like that? And why keep it low key? That's not like you."

Now that we'd shifted to a subject that LaForge enjoyed talking about, suddenly he had lots of time as he sat down on the arm of the couch next to the door to his office.

"India's too far," he explained. "You know me. I'm a hands-on guy. I've gotta be there a lot and I couldn't do that in India or someplace in Asia."

"Hands-on, or controlling?"

LaForge waved his hand in a dismissive motion.

"Doesn't matter either way. Mexicans work hard and they work cheap. It's close to the United States so I can get back and forth easily and the Mexican government gave us a lot of nice tax breaks and promise even more down the road, especially if we build another distribution center on the mainland, probably over on the gulf coast. There's no downside at all that I can see. As for the low-key part, outsourcing isn't popular in some quarters, especially among people who don't know anything about business but who do like to complain. And what does all this have to do with why I hired you anyway?"

It was my turn to make a dismissive gesture. "The more I know the better it is. The more connections I make the more likely it is that I can fix this thing."

LaForge nodded impatiently and walked out of his office to his secretary's desk just outside the door.

"Linda, I'll be gone a couple of hours," he said. "If the governor calls, tell him I'm out."

The instruction was pure ego. If he was, in fact, out, what else was she going to say? LaForge was just showing off.

As he walked away, she turned toward me so her boss couldn't see her and rolled her eyes.

I had no idea what she meant by that, but I had the feeling that I agreed with her.

CHAPTER 7

I SPENT the rest of the day in a conference room with Mort Bergman, LaForge's second in command, going over the information that LaForge left, plus a lot more.

By the time we finished my blazer was thrown over a chair, my tie was undone and my sleeves were rolled up to my elbows. Some of what I saw and heard was mildly interesting and some of it bored the eyeballs out of my head but none of it helped me.

Bergman was balding but not bad looking in a professorial way. In contrast to his boss, he always looked rumpled no matter what he wore or how expensive it was, although he seemed to have taken more care with his appearance than I remembered. He probably worked a minimum of sixty hours a week. His wife, Jane, was an elementary school vice principal. If they had a social life outside of what their jobs demanded no one was aware of it. As far as anyone knew, Mort Bergman's life was his work and his work was his life.

If Bergman was any good at self-promotion he would have gone off on his own by now. Word was that he wasn't paid nearly as well as someone in his position should be and LaForge treated him more like a flunky than a valuable number two in a fabulously successful, cutting-edge business. Although he apparently loved what he did, he was running out of time to run his own show and he was smart enough to know it. But maybe he didn't want his own show? A lot of people don't.

By the time we finished, even Bergman looked tired and bored. He took off his rimless glasses and rubbed the bridge of his nose with his thumb and index finger. The glasses left little indentations on each side of his nose.

"I don't know if Jeff mentioned this, but I will," he said. "I know you can't look into what's going on without talking to people and asking questions, but we'd appreciate it if you could keep it on the QT as much as you can. The word isn't out yet and we'd like to keep it that way. I don't know where all this will lead, but at the very least it'll be a distraction. Besides, maybe that's what whoever it is wants. Most people who do something like this just want attention."

"*We'd* appreciate it, or *you'd* appreciate it?" I asked. "Jeff being Jeff, I'm not sure he'd mind if the whole world knew. 'Courageous mogul carries on despite death threats.' What a guy!"

"You know what I mean," Bergman said quietly, the way he said everything. "Maybe sometimes it doesn't matter what Jeff thinks. Maybe he's not always right."

That was the closest I'd ever heard him come to criticizing his boss and it surprised me. Although it would be impossible to do my job and keep it a secret, I promised not to march around with an elephant and a brass band. It seemed to satisfy him.

It was early evening by the time I left the building. I sat in my rental car and went through the day's email on my phone. A couple of weeks ago, an older couple had asked me to look into their son's financial condition and this morning sent another email thanking me for my speedy work. The son, a sergeant in the army, kept writing to ask for money to help pay for his daughter's operations. I knew the son was lying about the medical expenses if not the operations themselves because as government dependents he and his family were provided medical care. He was making up hardship stories to bilk money out of his parents and it wasn't hard to prove. A little research revealed that he was gambling too much and owed a lot of money to a lot of people. When I explained what their son was up to, the parents were so devastated that I wished I hadn't found anything.

Not for the first time, I realized that the problem with looking under rocks is what you find there.

CHAPTER 8

I WENT BACK to my room at the Hyatt. My flight didn't leave until tomorrow afternoon and I contemplated having a drink in the lounge.

I was still contemplating when the telephone rang.

It was Mort Bergman.

"Ethan, you'd better come back here," he said. "One of our people was shot."

Bergman explained that his name was Jimmy Hopper. He was a photographer who shot a lot of the photographs that went into Focus, along with a lot of other stuff for the company; product shots, photos for the annual report, things like that. I knew who Hopper was without really knowing him, a wisecracking little guy who must have been forty and still looked like he was in his twenties, although he was married and had two kids.

I knew that Hopper was pals with Abby LaForge, too, a friendship that started before she met Jeff and continued after their marriage. At one time, there were rumors that they were more than just friends, but there were rumors about Abby and practically every man she ever met. After the other day, for all I knew there already were rumors about me, too. Or might be. Only this time, the rumors would be true.

After repeating the badge routine with the ever-vigilant Bernie, I met Bergman in his office. It was next to LaForge's office but about half the size.

"You think this is related to what I'm working on?" I asked.

"I dunno," Bergman admitted. "But I figured I'd better call you. I'm going to Memorial hospital. They're operating on Jimmy now."

"Where's Jeff?" I asked.

"I got him on his cell phone just before I called you," he said. "He'll probably come in here and then go to the hospital."

Bergman drove a new Saab convertible. I was surprised. It seemed like a dashing car for the Mort Bergman I knew. Dressing better and driving a snappy car? Was this the middle-age crazies I saw before me? I remembered a joke some female comedian used to make; whenever she saw a middle-aged man in a sports car she was always tempted to shout, "Sorry about your penis, sir." On the other hand, for all I knew maybe he got tired of dressing like an absent minded professor and just happened to be driving his wife's car today.

He filled me in on the way to the hospital, although he didn't know much. He got a call from the police that one of his people was down in Oxnard, south of Ventura near a new park, about a twenty-minute drive away.

The area around the park was known as La Brava, a mix of poor Asians, whites and Latinos. Most of the houses were too close together and in desperately bad shape, just like everything else in the area. The doors sagged, the screens had gaping holes when there were any screens at all, and paint peeled off the sides in large sheets. The streets were badly in need of repair, covered with potholes and laced with cracks that the city never got around to patching. It was a rare night when gunfire wasn't heard somewhere in the area.

The Projects were La Brava's most recognizable landmark - a half-dozen red brick apartment buildings that started as post-World War II housing. Each three-story building stretched for a half block with multiple entrances along the front, shaded by giant oak trees. The trees offered relief from the sun but killed the grass. Sometime in the sixties the apartments were converted into low-income housing, but like most such conversions it never had a chance. No one who intended to make a better life for themselves wanted anything to do with the Projects. Among its other charms, it was the vice capital of the county. Late at night, not even the police liked to go in there.

The few hardy families who fought to hold back the tide of sewage around them with neat houses and yards lived behind chain link fences and with steel bars across their windows and doors. They probably didn't go out much at night either.

The one bright spot was a new park recently opened by the city thanks to a federal grant. The playground equipment was bright and shiny and none of it was broken yet. The grass was green and the newly planted trees would grow and provide shade one day. There was a small gazebo in the center of the park and a fountain bubbled happily nearby. The park was maybe two blocks square, and sparkled like an emerald on black velvet. With the mayor standing beside him, an extremely self-satisfied congressman cut a ribbon during the opening ceremony and never came back. There weren't many votes to be had in La Brava.

As he made the turn into the hospital parking lot,

Bergman explained, "I have no idea what Jimmy was doing there. Maybe he was free-lancing. He did that a lot."

The only thing we knew for sure was that somebody shot him.

CHAPTER 9

WE ENTERED Memorial Hospital through automatic sliding doors that made a little hiss as they opened and closed.

Bergman went up to the desk, identified himself, and explained that one of his employees had been brought to the emergency room. The gray-haired lady behind the counter checked her computer and said that Hopper was in surgery, but his wife should be in one of the waiting areas on the sixth floor.

"A police detective is here, too," she said. "He might be with Mrs. Hopper now. That's where he said he was going."

We took the elevator to the sixth floor and stepped into the hallway. Other than a faint mechanical humming noise in the background, the place was mostly silent, the way hospitals always are once you get away from the lobby. The smell hit me first. I've never run into it anywhere else, but it exists in every hospital I've ever been, a combination of sickness, anxiety and other things I couldn't identify.

We checked at the desk in the Intensive Care Unit. A young nurse with her dark hair tightly pulled back behind her head directed us down the hall to a U-shaped alcove. The couches and chairs lining the walls were covered in aging light green vinyl. The windows across the rear wall overlooked the back of the hospital, which was mostly card-access staff parking.

A slim red-haired woman wearing Nike running shoes and a sleeveless black blouse tucked into Levis jumped up from a chair and ran into Bergman's arms. Her freckled face was pale and tear-streaked, but she was fighting to hold it together.

"Oh, Mort." Her voice was muffled by Bergman's chest. "He's still in surgery."

Tom Hauser was standing by the entrance to the alcove with a paper cup of coffee in his hand. He was wearing a blue jacket, tan pants and a long-sleeved white shirt with no tie.

This didn't seem like the time to introduce myself to Hopper's wife. I left her in Bergman's care and jerked my head at Hauser to step out into the hall.

"What are *you* doing here?" I asked.

"I heard about it," he said. "It happened in Oxnard, but he works for LaForge so I thought I'd check it out."

"You think this is related to what's going on with LaForge?" I asked.

"We're both here, aren't we?" he said.

Hauser had already talked to the EMTs who brought Hopper to the hospital. He was unconscious when they found him. He was shot twice, once in the small of his back and once in the back of the head. It looked like a small caliber handgun at close range.

"Small caliber as in a twenty two?" I asked.

"Don't know for sure yet, but probably," Hauser said.

"It doesn't have to be linked to the threats against LaForge," I said. "Maybe Hopper was just in the wrong place at the wrong time? In that area, it could be anything."

"Yeah, I know," said Hauser, looking around for a place to dump his half-empty cup of machine coffee. "Even if he makes it, who knows how long it'll be before he can talk, if he can talk at all, or even if he saw anything?"

Hauser walked over to a trash can beside the elevator, dumped his coffee in it, licked a little off his fingers, and walked back.

"What about the park?" I asked. "Anybody see anything?"

Hauser shook his head. "The Oxnard guys said no. In La Brava, nobody ever sees anything. Just before dark, a patrol saw a stripped down car that wasn't there earlier. He called it in, found out that it was the company car that Hopper usually drove, looked around a little and found Hopper not too far away."

We looked in on Bergman and Hopper's wife. She'd broken down and was softly crying on his shoulder while he patted her on the back. Poor Bergman looked as awkward as I felt.

I told Hauser that I had to get out of here.

"Sounds good to me," he said.

"Can you give me a ride?" I asked. "My car's back at LaForge's office."

I motioned to Bergman that we were leaving. His scowl told me that he wasn't pleased to be left alone. I didn't blame him.

Hauser's unmarked Ford was parked in a handicapped spot in front of the hospital. We rode in silence for a while. Being an exceptionally manly bastard, I didn't deal very well with grief. Right now I had too much of my own.

"All things considered, I'd say we handled it pretty well," Hauser said.

"You mean how we ran away the first chance we got?"

He nodded. "Something like that."

Hauser dropped me off at my car. As I opened the door to get out, he asked, "You going over to the park?"

"Yeah."

"I thought you might, even in the dark," he said. "I'll talk to you later."

I got in my rental as Hauser drove away. The traffic gods were with me, and it didn't take long to get to La Brava. I parallel parked in a spot across the street from the park entrance and walked over to where the EMTs found Hopper. Not far away, the fountain bubbled merrily. It was as if nothing had happened.

I didn't know if Hopper was entering the park, or coming out of it. If he'd already shot something, it might be good to see what he shot. I hadn't thought to ask about Hopper's equipment.

I walked along the sidewalk on both sides of the park entrance. Then I walked into the park, trying to imagine the circumstances of the shooting. Whatever Hopper was going to shoot probably had something to with the fountain. That would be the natural place for a photo. Coming up from behind would have been easy. I didn't know if whoever shot him was white, black, Asian or green. I didn't know if what happened was premeditated or spur of the moment. I didn't know if was related to the case I was supposed to be working on either, although Hauser was right, it probably was. Basically, I didn't know anything.

I looked around for Hopper's car. Hauser said that it hadn't been hauled away yet. The white Chevy Malibu was parked a block away from the park entrance.

In the speedy and efficient manner of the inner city, the car's tires were gone, the trunk and hood gaped open, the driver's side window was shattered, the door was hanging open and the radio was gone. Whoever did it could have broken into the car, started it in any one of several ways and driven away at their leisure, but it wouldn't have been as much fun as the simple joy of destruction. There was no point in trying to get finger-prints. By now half the kids in the neighborhood had their grubby little hands all over the car. To a little kid, there's something irresistible about an abandoned car.

I slowly walked around the park perimeter. Even if I didn't know what I was looking for, it didn't hurt to look. By the time I got back to my car, I had company.

There were two of them lounging against the driver's side of the rental with their backsides against the doors. Their body language spoke volumes, all of it insulting. They were in their late teens or early twenties and wore the uniform of the street, or the hood, or whatever it was called this week - gray hoodies, with baggy jeans down around their hips, the better to provide a scintillating view of their underwear, plus a variety of fascinating tattoos no doubt fraught with meaning. One was white and the other was Latino. Unless they had a gun some-where in their pants, which had enough room to conceal a bazooka, they were unarmed. But a gun is heavy and probably would have made their pants fall down. I didn't know what kept them up anyway. They seemed to defy gravity.

They looked at me. I looked back.

"It's good to see such a shining example of racial harmony in this fair city," I said.

The Latino was the spokesman of the pair. I could tell when he said, "Shut the fuck up, you stupid moth-erfucker."

I didn't know if they intended to roust me, rob me, steal my car, or sell me a time-share. I didn't care. I hadn't shaken my sour feeling from the hospital. The sight of Jimmy Hopper's wife wouldn't get out of my head. I didn't even stay long enough to learn her name.

I stepped up to the dynamic duo and hit the spokesman in the throat with a hard right. Grabbing at his throat, he slid down the side of the car, making a kind of moist choking sound as he fell.

The other one pondered the unexpected turn of events for about a nano second, then turned and ran like hell. Whatever they were planning, my rude gesture seemed to thwart it.

I kicked the one I hit out of the way, got in the rental and drove away. When I looked in the rear view mirror I could see him lying on the street. There was no sign of the other one.

Like Father Flanagan said, there's no such thing as a bad boy.

CHAPTER 10

"You felt bad about the hospital, so you took it out on those kids in the park," Dina said.

"I *did* feel bad about the hospital, but they weren't kids and I'm pretty sure they weren't after a donation to the Sierra Club," I said. "Are you suggesting I should make the day complete and look for an old dog to kick?"

She smiled. It was her patient smile, the kind that says, "I know I'm married to a dolt, but I love him anyway."

Since Dina died, I had conversations like this with her pretty often. A lot of people might have found it alarming. I didn't care.

"I'm not being judgmental," she said. "I just want to know how you're doing. Maybe you should see the doctor? It might help."

I'd driven back to my hotel from the park, drank a beer from the mini-bar in about eighteen seconds and took another one with me when I took a shower. Drinking beer in the shower is not a refined habit. Noel Coward probably never did it in his life. But Dina never seemed to mind except when I forgot and left the empty bottle on top of the shower stall. Even I had to admit that it looked a little tacky.

After calling Bergman to check on Hopper's condition, I sat and drank the remains of my second beer. I wasn't in a bad mood exactly, but I wasn't happy with myself either. Dina was pressing me to talk about it. I appreciated what she was trying to do, but at the same time it irritated me because I didn't want to, which is exactly why she was pressing me.

"How can you be so sure they didn't have something to do with what happened to Jimmy Hopper?" Dina asked.

"It's nothing I can explain," I said. "I just know it. They were two punks who thought they were tougher than they were, or I'd be easier than I was."

"Does the shooting have anything to do with LaForge?" she asked.

"Probably," I said.

"How is the one who was shot?" she asked.

"It doesn't look good," I said. "He's out of surgery but it's fifty-fifty at best. Even if he lives, he won't be in good shape."

"Brain damage?"

"Yeah. Spinal damage from the shot in the back, too. The surgeon told Bergman that even if he makes it he'll never fully recover."

"How's his wife doing?"

"How would you be doing?"

She reached across the table and squeezed my hand. Or at least she would have if she was still alive.

CHAPTER 11

I TOOK my usual place in his office, in an overstuffed chair across the small room from where he always sat. My chair was more comfortable than his. I assumed he set it up that way. A new replica of an old fashioned roll-top desk faced the wall opposite the window. The shades were drawn and it felt cool and comfortable in the semi-darkness.

"So tell me what's happening?" he asked.

"A lot," I said. "It's been an interesting few days. That's why I wanted to see you in person instead of talking on the phone. I appreciate you getting me in."

He acknowledged my thanks with an almost imperceptible nod of his head. "I assumed there was something unusual. Why don't you tell me about it?"

I told him everything from my first telephone conversation with LaForge to Jimmy Hopper's death and what happened in the park.

His eyes widened and he let out a deep sigh. "You're right. That *is* a lot."

His voice was the way it always was, calm and reassuring. He never scolded or judged. There was no guilt or innocence, right or wrong. Talking to him, it was as if there were no absolutes, only what we'd done, what we are, and what we want to be.

"How do you feel?" he asked.

I knew the question was coming. He asked it every session. I never had an answer prepared because I didn't trust myself to give an honest answer unless I was pushed. I usually discovered how I felt at the same time he did. Sometimes I didn't know how I felt and we worked it out together. I was often surprised at what we found.

My mother and father were murdered when I was a little boy and I saw it happen. They found me covered with my parents' blood a day or two later. Although I saw it, I've never been able to remember what happened that night, except sometimes in my nightmares, and I don't know if that's really how it happened. The result is that I have occasional episodes of disassociation where my consciousness shuts down but everything else keeps going. Afterward, I don't remember what happened and there have been times that what happened wasn't good. That's why I see a psychiatrist. Before Dina died, he said that the key to my therapy might be to somehow induce me to remember what happened the night my parents were murdered in their own home. We've tried everything, including hypnosis. A couple of times it seemed so tantalizingly close that it hurt. But I still wasn't able to break through. Since moving to Cabo San Lucas I'd only talked to the psychiatrist on the telephone because I didn't want to start all over with somebody new. Since Dina's death, we talked a lot more often.

There was a big aquarium next to the desk and the rhythmic bubbling sound it made was soothing. I put my head back against the chair and closed my eyes.

"I'm not sure how I feel," I admitted. "Mixed, I guess. I like it that LaForge came to me for help. That's pretty satisfying. But it created a lot of turmoil, too. Sometimes it's harder than I thought it would be, and sometimes it's easier."

"Turmoil how?" he asked. "Do you mean internally, or regarding the case?"

"A lot of both, but I meant internally. The internal stuff is why I'm here."

"Have you had any more episodes since the last time we talked?"

I shook my head.

"I haven't even had any symptoms lately," I said. "At least I don't think so."

If I felt the disassociation coming sometimes I could stop it, but only sometimes. At least I'd learned to recognize the symptoms. I might feel like I was going into a trance, or just disoriented. At other times everything would slow down and I'd get a tingling sensation in my scalp. If it was really bad I might have trouble understanding people, as if I couldn't focus on the words. Then there were times when I'd say something and didn't know where it came from, as if someone else said it, or I'd feel removed from everything around me, as if I was watching myself from a distance.

"Why do you think you took this case?" he asked.

"What do you mean? It's what I do."

He smiled. He was used to knocking down the barriers I put up.

"You know very well what I mean. This is going to press all the buttons you have and you knew it when you took it. It won't be easy. In fact, it may be very difficult. So why did you take it? Have you ever wondered why you don't like LaForge?"

"For one thing, he's a jerk," I said. "But I bet that's not what you're after, is it?'

"He may, in fact, be a jerk as you say, but what did he do to make you dislike him so much?"

"Have you been talking to my wife?" I joked. "That's the kind of thing she'd ask."

He just looked at me, his face set in neutral.

"Yeah, I know. She's been dead for more than a year. I still talk to her sometimes, though. It helps. I'm pretty sure I already told you that."

"You did and at the time I said it was all right. It was a way for you to process grief. But enough time has passed that the mourning needs to end, perhaps not right away, but soon. Remember, we're trying to get at why you feel the way you do and keep you from repeating certain patterns in your behavior. We have to be careful, here, Ethan. With your parent's death, Dina's death, and even with the death of your dog, you've lost everyone you've ever loved. That's not easy for anyone."

I thought about it for a while. He was comfortable with silence and didn't say anything to push me along.

"If I'm going to have a whole life that means sometimes I'll have to do things I don't want to do with people I don't like," I said "Running away won't help. It might even hurt."

"I'm not sure that's always the case," he said. "When you put it that way there's too much at stake. It becomes a challenge and only adds to the pressure you already feel. There are times when running away is the wise thing to do. You wouldn't think less of yourself if you ran away from a fire or a flood, would you?"

"You're right and I know it, but there it is anyway," I said. "I never said I was smart."

"On the contrary, you're very smart," he said. "That's part of the problem. You're too elusive. You're very good at finding reasons to repress your feelings and then denying that you're repressing them at all. But eventually they build up until they're released in one of your episodes, perhaps in a major episode. That's what we want to avoid."

"Okay, I get it."

"Do you? This case will go on and play out on its own. It's not something you can control. But the mourning is very in your control, especially after all this time. Do you think that Dina would want you to mourn forever?"

I smiled at that.

"You know, we used to talk about it sometimes. What if something happened to one of us? She said that I should be sad, but not for too long."

"Be sad, but not for too long," he repeated. "That's exactly right."

We talked for the rest of the hour. By the time I left his office I felt better. I almost always did, even when we just talked on the telephone. Sometimes I felt like I was getting close. But as the days passed that feeling always slipped away until next time.

Or maybe I was just fooling myself. But even if I was, I'd learned a long time ago that if I thought something helped, then it helped.

Sometimes there's a lot to be said for fooling yourself.

CHAPTER 12

THE TELEPHONE on the bedside table jangled me awake. My first thought was that I was supposed to go back to Cabo this afternoon. I was looking forward to it. If I liked Southern California I'd still live here.

It was Bergman. "Jimmy Hopper died this morning."

The funeral was two days later.

I hate funerals. I've only been to a couple, but I hate them anyway. I've never understood the point. The dead are beyond caring and most of the time it only makes the living feel worse.

Hopper was a popular guy and the funeral parlor was jammed. They had to put metal folding chairs in the aisles and across the back. His pretty red-haired wife looked unfocused and empty, as if she had no emotions left. She'd stare off into empty space and suddenly jerk back to attention. Hopper's mother, who looked like an older female version of her son, took charge of the two little kids. She didn't look so good herself. Your son isn't supposed to die before you do. His father sat rigidly at his wife's side, staring straight ahead, saying nothing, and looking uncomfortable in his suit and tie.

I took a seat on one of the folding chair in back, the

better for a fast getaway. Jeff LaForge was prominent in the second row, just behind the family, with Mort Bergman directly behind him. LaForge wore his grief like well-tailored clothes. It wasn't an emotion as much as an accessory.

The preacher, or holy man, or whatever he was, said all the usual things over occasional loud sniffles from the mourners. When he finally shut up, the organ music swelled and Hopper's mother rose to take the kids away. They didn't look scared or unhappy. They looked bewildered. People lined up to console the widow, who looked like she might collapse any second. For the second time in just a few days I decided that she didn't need to hear anything I had to say and went outside. I was mad at the world, but the world didn't give a damn.

Hauser was standing on the gray flagstone walk leading from the funeral parlor to the street. I'd spotted him on one of the aisle chairs during the service. He wore a dark blue suit, a gray-and-white patterned tie, a white shirt, and black wing-tip shoes. He'd loosened his tie the minute he got out into the open air.

He nodded when I walked up. I shook my head, blinking at the bright sunlight after being indoors. I reached inside my coat pocket, found my Ray Bans, and put them on.

"Hell of a thing isn't it?" he said. "I never get used to it."

"Christ, who'd want to?" I said

Mourners slowly filed out of the funeral parlor. They either stood around and talked in small clusters or headed to their cars for the drive to the cemetery.

It was a muggy afternoon, at least for Southern California. I took off my coat and held it over my shoulder with my index finger. Unlike Hauser, I didn't loosen my tie. Of course, my shirt collar wasn't strangling me either.

In the practiced way of a veteran cop, Hauser's eyes moved from face to face as the mourners walked past, registering everything for future reference. You never know who might show up at a funeral, even a killer. I heard a siren wail somewhere in the distance.

"By the way, the Oxnard PD got a complaint about somebody beating up on two guys in the La Brava park at about the same time you were out there," he said, looking over my shoulder as he talked. "You didn't happen to see anything, did you?"

"The world is a dangerous place," I said. "And everything in it unusual."

"That sounds like a quote," Hauser said.

"It probably was," I said. "I just can't remember who I'm quoting."

"It was dangerous enough for one of 'em," he said. "It'll be a while before he can talk. He got a bruised larynx from taking a shot in the throat."

"Did they get a description?"

Hauser's gaze shifted to look me in the eye. He probably would have grinned if we hadn't been standing outside a funeral parlor.

"Not really, except that he was white and seemed really pissed off," he said. "At least it'll keep the one guy's yap shut for a while. Both of 'em are regular customers of the Oxnard PD. I'm afraid they weren't shown a lot of sympathy."

It ended there. Hauser made it clear that he knew what happened, if not why, but that nothing would come of it. At the same time, I expressed my appreciation of the subtle nuances of law enforcement.

We watched as Jeff emerged from the funeral parlor, stopping at a group that included the mayor and at least one state senator. There were probably other political types around but I just didn't recognize them.

Nothing like a funeral to show how much you care about voters.

"Talk to LaForge today?" Hauser asked.

I shook my head. "Haven't had a chance."

My cell phone vibrated. When I saw the text, I said, "Oh, shit."

"What's wrong?" Hauser asked.

"It's from Abby, Jeff's wife down in Cabo," I said. "She got another love note. She's sending it. Hang on."

When it arrived, it was a photo of simple, blue-lined notebook paper with perforations along the left edge. The words "YOUR NEXT" were scrawled across the page in capital letters.

"Nice spelling, Hauser said.

I held my cell phone in my hand and stared at the image like I expected it to burst into flame under my relentless gaze.

"I've gotta get back," I said. "I've stayed here too long. This is your turf. Cabo's mine."

"You better tell LaForge," Hauser said. "Here he comes."

I showed LaForge what I had, watched his eyes widen, and told him that I was headed back to Cabo on the first flight I could catch.

He shook his head. "Let's both go down on the corporate jet. It's right here in Oxnard. We can leave as soon as we get to the airport."

As much as I didn't want to travel with LaForge, that was the best thing do to. After agreeing to meet at the tiny Oxnard airport, I went back to my hotel, got my stuff, and drove to the airport, where I paid a surcharge to turn in my rental there instead of where I picked it up in Los Angeles. Since the charge went to LaForge, I didn't care.

The flight to Cabo was a breeze. I was a fan of private

jets. Security leaving the U. S. and entering Mexico was as simple as it was perfunctory. There was no standing in line at the gate and somebody else handled the luggage. A red-haired flight attendant whose name tag said she was Ginger served us food and drink. We were met at the Cabo airport by a driver from LaForge's company, who drove a company Hummer like a bat out of hell to LaForge's house on the beach, where we arrived only a little more than two hours after we left the funeral.

Abby greeted us at the door and hugged us both at once. She wore knee-length blue shorts and a white top with short sleeves. She looked angry more than frightened and made anger look awfully good.

"You okay, babe," LaForge asked, holding her hand.

She nodded. "Yeah, I'm fine. It'll take a lot more than some illiterate note to get to me."

We went out back and sat down by the pool and cabana. I stirred uneasily in my chair, all too aware of what took place here just a few days ago.

"How did you find the note, Abby?" I asked.

"I went out to do some shopping, down in that mall near the marina where the designer shops are. It took maybe an hour. When I went back to the car I found the note under the wiper. At first I thought it was a flyer. You get 'em in parking lots all the time. I almost threw it away without looking at it. When I saw what it was I took a picture of it with my cell phone and called you."

"Why the hell didn't you call me?" LaForge asked with considerable indignation.

"I dunno," Abby admitted. "I didn't think it through. I mean, after all, *he's* the detective. I just figured that he ought to know right away."

LaForge took her hand again, looking concerned. But I could tell that he was stewing because he wasn't first choice.

"See anybody hanging around your car or in the parking lot when you arrived?"

"No, but I wasn't looking. There's was nobody close, though."

"See anybody watching after you read the note?"

"I did look around then but I didn't see anything. Nobody was doing anything obvious that I could tell."

"No cars leaving in a hurry? Nobody walking away? Nobody staring at you from a distance? Nobody sitting in a car and watching?"

Abby shook her head again. She was getting irritated, too.

"Look, Ethan, I said I didn't see anything." Her voice was harder than before. "It was a parking lot. Cars came and went. So did people. Nobody seemed to be staring or doing anything out of the ordinary. That's all I can tell you."

I held up my hand in apology.

"Sorry to seem to be riding you. But I had to ask. You know that. Have you told the Cabo police yet?"

She shook her head. "I know I should have called 'em right away, but I haven't."

"That's okay. I'll do it. Do you have the note?"

Abby went inside the house and brought it back, holding it by the edge with two fingers as if she didn't want to soil her hands with it.

"The Cabo police will have some questions and probably come out here. It'll be the same kind of thing I asked. Just keep your temper in check and tell 'em what you know."

I called Valencia. He said that he would come himself. There was no reason for me to stick around so I didn't.

But I did leave the house with information that I didn't have before. It was a sure thing that Jeff and Abby LaForge were being watched. Nobody accidentally saw her in a parking lot and decided to leave her a threatening note for the hell of it. That the note said she was next told me that whoever left it knew about Jimmy Hopper and maybe had something to do with his shooting, even if they just knew about it. There might be more than one person involved, too. Unless they got around awfully fast.

I didn't know why and I didn't know who, but at least I had something new. I take progress wherever I can find it.

CHAPTER 13

I NEEDED TO WORK OUT. I drove home, changed clothes and went down to the La Gaviota tennis club in Cabo to see if I could pick up a match.

Three guys I barely knew needed a fourth and we started playing on the clay courts. About halfway through the second set something happened. The next thing I knew I had my fingers laced through the chain link fence at the back of the court and my racquet was shattered and broken in my other hand. I was breathing hard and I had no idea how I got there or how long it had been.

I turned around, blinking like I'd just come into bright sunlight. It happened so fast there were no symptoms for me to recognize. The three other guys were standing by the net, staring like I'd just beamed in from Pluto. Nobody said a word.

I felt tired and empty. I walked to the bench beside the net to get my bag and dropped what was left of my racquet in the plastic trash container at the side of the court.

"I'm sorry," I said. "It's been kind of a bad few days. I better not play anymore. I apologize for ruining the match."

I stopped at the desk inside to arrange to pay for the round of drinks I knew that the other three guys would have so they could talk about me. Without looking back, I walked to the locker room, ripped off my clothes and sat naked in the steam room with my head down for as long as I could stand it. I liked it there because when the steam was thick enough I couldn't see anybody else. Somebody said something through the clouds but I didn't answer.

The storm had passed, but I didn't want to face people. I showered and went home without a word. I was supposed to call the psychiatrist with something like this happened, but I didn't want to see or talk to anyone. I was tired of gazing at my own navel. I decided to read instead. I was working on Robert Caro's gigantic "The Years of Lyndon Johnson: The Passage of Power." After I finished it would make a nice doorstop. I'd wanted to learn more about Johnson ever since Dina and I visited the Johnson library in Austin a couple of years ago. It beat the hell out of the Ronald Reagan library in Simi Valley. We agreed that it had something to do with the fact that the Johnson library was affiliated with the University of Texas, while the Reagan library was a stand-alone operation. The Reagan library was a shrine, while the Johnson library had meaning and purpose beyond itself. It offered a sense of context that showed Johnson as he was, not some idealized version that grew more and more distant from the real thing as time passed.

The more I read the more it seemed to me that Caro probably didn't like his subject. I didn't blame him. In a lot of ways Johnson was a loathsome human being. I wondered what it would be like to spend years researching and writing about someone you didn't like? Did the benefits outweigh the possibility that it might curdle your soul after a while? For Caro, I guess it did.

Maybe he knew something I didn't? There was a lot of that going around.

I fell asleep while I was reading. By the time I woke up it was as if I'd dreamed what happened on the tennis court. That made it easier to pretend that it didn't happen at all.

I was supposed to meet Valencia for dinner. I needed some help and Valencia said that he had just the man for me. To make it less formal, we arranged a meeting tonight. I dressed, left the house without bothering to put the top up on the Mustang and headed to Villa Serena, a few minutes away just outside of Cabo. I wore a dark blue polo shirt, tan pants and sandals. I drove toward Cabo, turned left onto a nondescript dirt road that looked like it didn't go anywhere even when you were on it, had my teeth rattled by the ruts, and parked beside the restaurant. There were only four cars in the lot but that didn't mean it was a slow night. A lot of Cabo tourists don't rent cars. If they're staying in town, they can walk wherever they want to go. If it's too far – and Villa Serena was – taxis, most of them vans, are plentiful.

As I stepped through the door, I spotted Valencia at the bar with a young roly-poly looking guy. They saw me at about the same time. Valencia said something to the bartender and slid off the stool. With his white linen shirt and trousers and dashing looks, he looked like a gigolo, except that most gigolos don't look that good.

Valencia held up his drink: My guess was vodka tonic, a good warm weather drink. The young guy had a Negra Modelo.

"They will put the drinks on the dinner bill," he announced. "Then I will tear up the bill. It is very convenient."

We were shown to our table. With a palapa roof, Villa Serena was open on three sides, including the one that faced the ocean, which was about a quarter of a mile away, with a few homes scattered between us and the water. There was a small swimming pool a couple of steps away from the restaurant, although I'd never seen anyone in it, not even a tourist who had too much to drink and fell in. It was about a half hour until sunset and you could already see a few lights out on the ocean, probably cruise ships making the run on what they called the Mexican Riviera.

Valencia introduced me to Ramon Garcia, who looked like he was in his mid-20s. He was about five feet, eight inches tall and maybe two hundred pounds, with the usual dark hair. He wore a white long-sleeved shirt with the sleeves rolled up on his forearms, dark trousers, and a black leather belt and dark loafers.

Shaking my hand across the table, he said, "Mister, uh, Crankshock, I am very happy to meet you."

I was used to getting my name butchered down here, just as I was sure that I butchered many Mexican names, but Crankshock? That was a new one.

I explained to Garcia that his duties were a little vague and we'd have to make it up as we went along. For the time being I wanted him to pose as a gardener working around the LaForge place and watch for anything out of the ordinary while he raked, trimmed, and mowed. Valencia could arrange everything with the landscaping company so that Jeff and Abby wouldn't know it.

"You want me to be a Mexican gardener?" Garcia asked, his jaw practically thumping on the floor. Clearly, acting out a cliché was not what he had in mind.

At that awkward point, we were saved by the waiter. I didn't need to look at the menu. Many years ago, when Dina and I first came to Cabo, the restaurant offered lobster for ten bucks. It still offered the lobster, but the ten buck days were long gone. It was still a good deal and I ordered a pre-dinner margarita, too. It would be, I was sure, the first of several. Both Valencia and Garcia ordered shrimp, plus another round of drinks.

While we waited for dinner, I told them almost everything that happened so far, concentrating on what happened since I left Cabo, which by now seemed like about five years ago. I say almost because I left out what happened between me and Abby. The fewer people who knew the better it was for both of us.

It was a two margarita story and I finished with my conclusion Jeff and Abby were being watched.

"It does seem that way," Valencia agreed, downing the last of his vodka and tonic. "But there's no proof that the notes had anything to do with the other man's death, even the last note. That murder could have been random and whoever is making the threats might be taking the opportunity to pretend he had something to do with it just to frighten LaForge a little more. I don't think so and neither do you. But there needs to make a connection and so far we don't have one."

As we ate and drank our way through dinner, I noted that the situation suffered from a manpower shortage, which was why I needed help. I was only one guy and Valencia didn't have enough people in his department to spend a lot of man hours watching Mister and Mrs. LaForge.

"I know that impersonating a gardener isn't exactly what you had in mind and it's not terribly original either," I explained to Garcia. "But in a place like the Palms those guys are such a common sight they're practically invisible. It's perfect. Besides, I'm not asking you to *be* a gardener, just to impersonate one for a while. Trust me, it will get better."

Garcia looked helplessly at Valencia, who only shrugged and said, "It's a good idea."

"For now, that's about it," I said. "Do you have a gun?"

Garcia glanced at Valencia.

"Yes," said Valencia, "he does."

"What is it?" I asked.

Another glance from Garcia at Valencia.

"A police issue Glock," replied Valencia. "While he's gardening, he can wear it in a shoulder holster under his shirt."

"Ramon, it's probably better if *you* answer my questions," I said.

"I know," Garcia admitted sheepishly. "Sometimes I rely too much on my *tio*."

"Your uncle?" I said, it being my turn to be surprised. "Valencia is your uncle?"

"I thought you knew," he said.

I looked at Valencia who looked back at me and smiled.

"Ramon, I don't want to offend you but are you sure you're up for this?" I asked.

"He has experience," Valencia said. "Some time with the Mexico City police. He showed much potential."

"'Shows potential' is another way of saying that he's young," I pointed out. "If he's so good why isn't he working?"

Garcia's palm slapped down on the table with a loud smack that caused several other diners to stare at us.

"Stop talking about me as if I'm not here," Garcia said, his dander rising high.

I liked that. He should be angry.

"Okay, you talk," I said. "What the hell are you doing here?"

Garcia explained that his future in law enforcement took an iffy turn in Mexico City when he threw his captain through a door.

I raised my eyebrows. "A door? Not a doorway?"

"We were having a, ah, heated discussion in the captain's office and the door was closed," Garcia said. "I ended the discussion by throwing him through it."

"Cheap modern construction," Valencia interrupted with a smile. "Where are the craftsmen of old?"

"The captain wound up with a broken collar bone," Garcia continued. "And I wound up getting fired."

"What happened to the captain?"

"May I answer," Valencia asked.

I nodded.

"The man is a pig. *Muy malo.* So naturally he now holds an appointed position high up in government."

"Naturally," I said, "what are pigs for if not to hold high positions in government. And you vouch for Ramon here?"

"He is eager, honest and smart. He is also here in Cabo and willing to work cheap."

This time Garcia interrupted his uncle.

"*Tio*, I agree with everything you said except the part about working cheap."

Once we all stopped laughing I decided that I liked young Garcia.

"Okay, I can use the help. I'll have to convince Jeff to pay the extra freight, but I'm guessing he will. It's just one guy."

By the time we finished we'd devoured everything in sight and I'd restricted myself to three margaritas. As with most drinks in Cabo, they were pretty light on the alcohol, the better to squeeze more drinks out of a bottle. When the check came, Valencia looked at the owner, who was behind the bar, dressed in a white shirt and bow tie. When the owner nodded, Valencia tore the check in half.

"That *is* a nice system," I said. "We should leave a good tip though."

"Considering that the dinner was free, *you* should leave a good tip," Valencia replied, rising from the table. "If you will excuse me, I have to go. I wish you luck."

"And I have to visit *los banos* on the way out," Garcia said.

"I don't," I said. "I'll call you when we've made arrangements for you new gig."

We shook hands and Garcia headed over to the bathroom near the bar while I counted out sufficient dollars – every business in Cabo took dollars in addition to the national currency – and tossed them on the table.

I walked out to the parking lot. The only light came from the half-moon and an underpowered fixture above the door. As I approached my Mustang, an old Ford Taurus with rust spots along the side molding came clattering up and slammed to a stop across the back of my car, blocking my way out. Three men emerged. One of them carried an aluminum baseball bat. I suspected that they were not from the local softball team.

I wasn't carrying a gun. I'd figured that I was having dinner with the chief of police in a nice restaurant. How much danger could there be? The three-part answer was headed my way.

My right hand was already in my pocket because I was reaching for my car keys when they pulled up. I pulled my hand out with the keys in it, the ignition key sticking out between my second and third fingers. The rest of the keys were clutched in my fist. My left hand was on the side away from my new friends, and I reached in my pocket and palmed a credit card.

"Hey, you!" The lead man had an accent I couldn't place. It was Spanish, but different, too. "*Vamos a hablar!*"

He said that he wanted to talk, but I had a much different impression. The slugger was a step behind the other two. He was about twice the size of his pals and grinned as he slapped the bat onto the palm of one hand.

I worked the credit card between my thumb and index finger. "Listen, if it's money you want, here …." I held my left hand out like I was handing something over and flicked the credit card at the lead man's eyes. It wasn't much, but it distracted him. I stepped forward with my left foot, came up hard with my right hand and jammed the key into the soft spot underneath his chin all the way to my knuckles. He staggered but didn't fall, hands clawing underneath his chin.

They'd planned badly. With his buddies between us, the bruiser with the baseball bat didn't have a clear shot. Even so, there still were more of them than there was of me. I shoved the guy with my keys hanging under his chin toward the other two. Suddenly all three went down in a heap as Garcia hit them like a cannonball right around the knees. He rolled through the motion and was back on his feet before they knew what hit them.

I got around in back of the second one. As he got to his feet I ran my arms through his armpits and clasped my hands at the back of his neck so that I had him in a full nelson. I bashed his face on the front window of my Mustang; once, twice, three times. When I felt him go limp I let him fall.

The first one was sitting on the ground with a dazed look on his face, my keys still dangling under his chin and blood dribbling out of his mouth. The slugger was face down on the ground. Garcia stood over him with the bat in one hand and the barrel resting on his shoulder. He looked like he was about to take batting practice. Whatever Garcia did, he did it for keeps. The slugger didn't even twitch.

With his free hand, Garcia unhooked his cell phone from his belt and made a call. The conversation was brief.

"I called my uncle. He had not gone far. A car will be here *una momento*. Are you all right?"

"Excuse me," I said.

I walked around to the other side of my car. I put one hand on the hood, bent over and threw up the dinner I'd finished a few minutes earlier. I was careful not to get any on my shoes.

"It's the adrenaline rush," Garcia said.

I stood up and wiped my mouth with the back of my hand.

"I think it had more to do with naked fear," I said. "But I like your explanation a lot better. By the way, I did mention that you're hired, didn't I?"

Garcia walked over to the guy who had my keys in his chin, bent down and looked him square in the face.

"Do you recognize them?" he asked.

I took a look. "Beats the hell out of me. As far as I know, I've never seen 'em before."

It took about thirty minutes to sort everything out with the police. Fortunately, Valencia came, too. Without him, it would have taken a lot longer.

An ambulance took the three men away, with one uniformed cop inside and another following in the squad car. I made sure to get my keys back before they left. I had to go into the restaurant bathroom and clean off the ignition key.

It wasn't until I got home that I realized I'd forgotten my credit card. It was probably still on the ground at the parking lot.

I was too tired to drive back to the restaurant. I called the credit card company and reported the card missing. The company promised to stop credit on the card I "lost" and to send another one immediately. I showered and went to bed. Brewster used to sleep with us every night.

In fact, he used to take up more of the bed than we did. I missed him.

CHAPTER 14

I WAS STILL ASLEEP when Valencia called early the next morning.

"That accent you couldn't place last night?" he said, "They are from Nicaragua. You have a good ear for a gringo."

My head was still gummy from being jarred out of sleep.

"Nicaragua? Okay, what else have you got?"

"Nothing," he said.

"Nothing?" I said.

"You are sharp this morning, aren't you?"

"You're not catching me at my best."

"I never do. They had no identification. We ran their prints but came up dry. I doubt that there will be any kind of record anywhere. The record keeping down there is less than spectacular."

"What were they after? It sure as hell wasn't a robbery."

"Their intentions were to rough you up and break something."

"That explains the baseball bat," I said. "But it doesn't explain why."

"They don't know why. They were just doing what they were told. They said someone they don't know paid three hundred American money, with another three hundred when they finished the job. Other than that they don't know a thing. I believe them. If you added up their IQs you wouldn't equal the room temperature. I doubt that we'll be able to find who hired them. Even if we did, it probably wouldn't matter. There's someone above him, too. The price probably started at two or three thousand and every level took a cut on the way down."

"Six hundred?" I said. "I think I'm insulted. What about the car?"

"Stolen, of course," he said. "Stealing a *cajada de mierda* like that shows you how smart they are."

"I think you just called their car a shit box. I can only agree. How was the mystery man behind it supposed to know they did the job? What kept them from doing nothing, saying they beat me up, and collecting the rest of the money?"

"A broken arm or leg would show, wouldn't it?"

"So far your investigation is not a comfort to me," I said.

"Give it time," he said. "We probably won't be a comfort then either. My nephew was a comfort last night, though."

"He could have just drawn his gun and saved the effort," I said. "Except, as I seem to recall, he wasn't armed."

"None of us were. As it turned out, it wasn't necessary. Still, if I were you, I would not go unarmed again until this thing is over."

I knew that I wouldn't get back to sleep. I showered, shaved, drank some coffee, scrambled some eggs, toasted a muffin, and filled a glass with orange juice. I took my laptop outside to the patio and went on line while I ate to see if there was anything new on Jimmy Hopper's murder. Apparently LaForge had posted a twenty five thousand dollar reward for information leading to the arrest of whoever did it. Fifty thousand would have been better, especially since it was no doubt corporate money, but Jeff was too cheap to go that high.

Valencia was right. After last night, it was a bad idea to go unarmed. Mexico has tough gun laws but I had a magic card from high up in the Mexican government giving me permission to carry a firearm and to do a lot of other things besides. It was better than a flying carpet.

We dress light in Cabo San Lucas so an ankle holster seemed the best choice. Fortunately, I had a good ankle rig. It had a compression strap designed to pull the gun butt tight against my calf, which gave the weapon a low profile and kept it secure in case I had to do any running. I own about twenty weapons that I've accumulated over the years, which is a lot more than I need. Most of them I keep at home, with a couple stored in a bank deposit box in Cabo and a couple more in a bank deposit box in Southern California. After perusing the inventory at home, I decided on a Sig Sauer P239. It was small enough to work with the holster, but still had some stopping power. The limited range was all right with me - I wasn't going to try to bag an elk at three hundred yards – and it only weighed two pounds with a full ten-round magazine.

I strapped on the ankle holster and slipped the Sig in it. I usually don't like an ankle rig. It's slower to get to than a shoulder holster and Dina said that the extra weight on one leg always made me walk like John Wayne after too many drinks. But I decided that it was best to put up with the inconvenience of a funny walk while avoiding fast-draw contests.

I checked my email and found a message from an

angry woman who wanted me to find her missing husband. She was friends with a client I had a few years back, a couple who'd signed a deal for a top to bottom remodel of their house. The contractor convinced them to pay most of the money in advance and then skipped with their hundred thousand dollars.

Finding a missing person is easier than most people think. High profile cases to the contrary, most missing children aren't really missing; they're lost. If they're genuinely missing, then usually an estranged husband or wife or angry relative took the child. Sometimes people disappear to avoid unpleasant realities. Most teenagers run away to escape from a problem that's too big for them to handle. An adult might run away from a spouse, from financial problems, a romance gone bad, trouble at work, or psychological problems. What helps people like me find them is that they still have to make a living. They change their address, but rarely change their profession. That's how I found the crooked contractor. He moved and formed a new company with a new name. His mistake was that he named himself president of the company. I tracked him through the State Contractor's Board. The fact that I was not dealing with a great criminal mind made my job a lot easier.

I emailed back to say that I was on a case full time and didn't know how long it would last. Besides, I didn't really do that kind of thing anymore. I recommended somebody else and warned her that even if her husband was found the coming back part was up to him.

She must have been on line because she emailed right back: "That's all right. I just want him found so that I can sue his worthless ass for divorce."

Just another reminder about why I didn't do that kind of thing anymore.

CHAPTER 15

MY NEXT MOVE was to have a long talk with Linda Giordano, LaForge's executive assistant, or whatever her title was, the one who rolled her eyes when he wasn't looking.

It's been my experience that someone in Giordano's position knows more than anybody about what was really going on, business and personal. I knew her a little, but only a little. During my day in the office with Mort Bergman, I'd learned that she'd been with LaForge for a long time, practically since the beginning. She must have started young because she looked at least ten years younger than he did. Her hair was light brown and she wore it in what used to be called a shag, I think. I had no idea what it was called now. She was tall, about five ten, attractive in a healthy, in-shape way, one of those people whose vitality makes them seem better looking than they really are, another way of saying that she was quite an attractive woman.

A little more research found that she was divorced. She was so valuable to LaForge's empire that she frequently traveled either with him or by herself on the corporate jet. She was good at her job and protective of her boss the way someone in her position should be, but didn't treat him like a hot-house flower either. She laughed at his pretensions, his big and little lies, his poses and exaggerations, and wasn't intimidated by his temper. When he didn't get his way, LaForge had a nasty, even vicious, temper. Linda usually ignored it, which seemed to irritate and bemuse him at the same time.

In short, she did her job without being slavish or toadying. Jeff LaForge was not an easy man to work for at the best of times, but considering the necessary intimacy of their relationship, Linda Giordano did it as well as anyone could. I would be astonished if they had anything going on, now or ever, although I had no doubt that LaForge tried. If nothing else, he'd try out of habit. I was pretty sure that Linda had better taste.

The whole thing might be a little tricky. I wanted to talk to her but I didn't want LaForge to know it, meaning that I didn't want her to tell him. We'd never developed beyond a lightly bantering relationship and I wondered if we still had one, although rolling her eyes at her boss while knowing I could see it gave me hope.

"Jeffrey LaForge's office."

"Linda, it's Ethan Cruickshank."

"Who?"

"Don't start torturing me already."

"But it's such fun!"

Okay, I thought, nothing has changed.

"I want to talk to you but I don't want Jeff to know it. If you're not okay with that I understand and I'll say no more, though I'd appreciate it if you wouldn't either. If you are okay with it then I'd like to meet."

After about ten seconds of silence that made me think that my bid had failed, she said, "You're in Cabo now, right?"

"Yes."

"I'm coming down there tomorrow morning."

"Great," I said. "How about dinner?"

"Will it be an expensive dinner?"

"Not if I can help it."

"You are not being very persuasive."

"I take it that Jeff's not nearby listening to your every word."

"Nope. He flew to Denver for a couple of days."

"So what about dinner?"

"Will you interrogate me and use a lot of old private eye tricks to get me to talk?"

"I have a bunch of new private eye tricks I'm dying to try out," I said. "Besides, I was hoping a glass of cheap wine might do just as well."

"You are so diabolical!"

"I'd better not pick you up since I don't want anybody to know we talked. How about if I meet you someplace? Do you know Cabo at all?"

"As long as we're not meeting at some hole in the wall, in which case I would be as silent as the Sphinx when we meet, I'll find it."

"Okay, how about the Galleon at seven tomorrow night?"

"I know it and I'll be there. Just remember that the more expensive the wine the more I'll have to say."

"You don't know what I want to talk about."

"Well, duh," she said with a laugh. "For some reason the word dirt comes to mind."

And with that, she hung up.

CHAPTER 16

I CALLED *El Galeon* and made reservations. Having been around for many years that had become decades, it was one of the few genuine upscale restaurants in Cabo, right down to the white linen tablecloths. Not your typical tequila-shots hotspot. Set on a hillside just below the Hotel Finisterra, it overlooks the city and the marina, where the four hundred or so boat slips were jammed, as usual, with a variety of sleek and mostly expensive craft. Supposedly the marina could accommodate boats of up to 375 feet. I wondered what it would be like to own a boat that was longer than a football field. I concluded that mostly it would be expensive.

El Galeon was one of the classiest restaurants in Cabo. I picked it because if everything went well, we'd be here a while and I wanted Linda to feel relaxed and comfortable.

The restaurant offered valet parking and I took advantage of it. I was just getting out of the Mustang when Linda showed up in a taxi. At that moment, she may have been the best-dressed person in Cabo, wearing a dark blue pantsuit with a fine chalk line and an ivory blouse with a gold chain showing at her throat.

We kissed each other on the cheek and went inside to be shown to the window table I'd requested. It was a warm night, but the restaurant was air conditioned so we had the best of both worlds, the world-class view without the humidity.

We made small talk for a few minutes while Linda figured out what to order. As I almost always did, I ordered the *osso buco*. Linda ordered a small Caesar salad, which they always prepared at the table, and veal marsala. I let her order the wine. As long as it didn't taste like Dr. Pepper, or something just as awful, I didn't particularly care. She ordered well. Not the cheapest and not the most expensive, but one of the best.

She smiled sweetly at my questioning look.

"It occurred to me that you're probably going to expense it out and the company will wind up paying for this," she said. "I'd do a lot more damage if we were spending your money."

"I can only imagine," I said.

"This is the first time I've ever had dinner with a, uh, sleuth," she said. "Tell me, are you carrying a gun?"

I was wearing the ankle rig. After glancing around the restaurant to make sure no one was looking, I stuck my leg out from under the table and lifted the leg of my pants just enough to let her see it. She beamed happily.

"Actually, I just like to show off my ankles," I said.

Unfortunately Linda had just taken a sip of wine. She started to giggle and the giggle turned into a serious choking sound.

The noise brought the waiter scurrying over. "*Senora*, are you all right?" he asked, leaning over the table with one hand on her back, poised to pound away and save her life.

Linda was coughing into her napkin and her eyes

were tearing, but she managed to raise a hand and wave him away.

Every eye in the restaurant was on us. Just like that, we'd become a spectacle. It took a few minutes before she recovered. The embarrassment was probably worse than the choking.

Finally, she took a deep breath. "Okay, I think I'll live. But it was close for a while."

"I think you were in pretty good hands with the waiter," I said.

"Are you kidding?" she said. "He'd have beaten me to death in the name of first aid."

Not wanting to be interrupted once we started, I waited until the food arrived before getting down to business.

"How much do you know about what's going on?" I asked.

"Most of it, I think," she said. "Tell me what I'm missing: Jeff hired you to investigate the threats, the bullets, the vandalism, the whole shot. Add to the mix what happened to poor Jimmy and that little dust up you got into in the restaurant parking lot."

"How did you know about that?"

"Jeff makes sure that we know what's going here, both officially and unofficially," she replied. "After all, we're already one of the biggest employers in Cabo, well on our way to becoming the biggest, and we *should* know, don't you think? Three against two. Not bad."

"Actually it was three against one," I said, wondering if I should tell Valencia that somebody on his police force was a source for Jeff LaForge. "The other guy held my coat while I dispatched the ruffians."

"Of course." She smiled another one of her sweet smiles that made me doubt her sincerity. "You must be very proud."

"You can't imagine," I said. "Okay, let's get started. You are my client's executive factotum, or whatever your title is, and a darned good one you are, too. As such, you undoubtedly know more about him than he would like, and maybe more than you would like. That means you are someone I should talk to, which explains our presence here."

"I work with Mort Bergman, too, in the same capacity," she said. "In effect, I'm the number three in the corporation, although they don't call me that and certainly don't pay me at that level."

"Really?" I said. "When did that happen?"

"A few months ago," she said, risking another sip of wine. "Our rapid expansion in the last couple of years has cost a lot of money. All the departments had to make cutbacks. One of them was Mort's factotum, as you say. She was leaving anyway and they didn't fill the position. They gave me a medium raise, a new title, and practically doubled my workload. Lucky me."

"I'm surprised at the cutbacks," I said. "I thought Jeff was ridiculously successful and becoming even more so."

She explained that when Jeff was interested in expanding into a new area, usually suppliers of what he sold on the internet, he preferred to buy an already successful company instead of starting from scratch himself.

"That gets us into whatever field very quickly and feeds Jeff's need for instant gratification at the same time," she said. "But it's also expensive as hell and we're showing the strain. The bottom line still looks okay but it's growth through acquisition and not genuine growth, which would be a lot healthier. We'll be all right in the long haul but for now Jeff is under considerable pressure. And by the way, that is *not* something that I want to go beyond this table. Call it context for your investigation."

In turn, I told her more or less about everything that had happened and what I'd learned so far. I trusted her more than the official private eye manual suggests that I should, but I believed her to be trustworthy. One way to get people to open up to you is to open up to them, or at least make them think so.

"As I see it, there are three possibilities," I said. "One is that some nutcase has fixed on LaForge. In that case, it isn't really personal. It could just as easily be Elvis Costello or the telephone company. Everything seems too persistent for that, but every case is different. If that's true it'll be a lot harder to figure out because it's so random and quirky. Another possibility is that it's one of the cops or ex-cops who might still be cranky about what happened years ago. Somebody else is looking into that one but we don't really think anything's there."

"And the last?"

"I keep coming back to Jeff's extracurricular activities," I said. "Husbands get jealous. Boyfriends, too. Sometimes they get mad. Sometimes they lose it altogether. He swears that's not the case, but how would he know? Jeff LaForge does not have a history of being attuned to the feelings of others. He also claims to have given up outside canoodling. For what it's worth, Abby says the same thing. And if any of this is related to Hopper or the guys who came after me, and I think it must be, I have no idea how."

"I love it when you say 'canoodling.'"

"I kind of liked it myself."

She smiled and took another small sip of her wine. In over a half hour she hadn't finished half of it. I suspected that she ordered it just for show and would have been just as happy with water or iced tea.

"So what you really want me to do is rat on my boss," she said.

"If you want to put it that way, yes, but only if there's something to rat," I said. "If there isn't, that could help too, maybe by eliminating one or more of the possibilities. That's what a lot of this business is about. The last one standing is the answer."

Linda gathered her thoughts while she cut at the veal with her fork. She was good at it. Not everyone had the skill of fork cutting. It's all in the wrist.

"Let me put it this way," she said. "I don't know if Jeff is faithful or not. I haven't heard anything to make me think something's going on, but I wouldn't necessarily know it if there was. But I think Abby's getting it on, and not just with her husband."

I gulped at that, not too obviously, I hoped. I was surprised by how sure she was. She had no doubt at all. And I really hoped that she wasn't talking about me.

"How about a little more specificity?" I said, worried that I was about to hear what I feared that I would.

"You mean names, dates and places?"

"Names for a start," I said.

"Names I don't have," she admitted. "Places and dates either. But I do know they argue. A lot, too."

"Jeff and Abby?"

Linda nodded.

"How do you know?"

"She calls him or he calls her the way husbands and wives and boyfriends and girlfriends do," she said. "All calls come through me, unless it's on Jeff's cell phone. Even when the calls about something else, just everyday stuff, they often have a way of getting around to that mysterious whatever it is that starts the argument. One time he called her a slut. I believe 'fucking slut' is the exact quote. The arguments are getting more and more intense and happen more often. If what I hear is any indication, their home life must be hell on wheels."

"If what you say is true, then Abby lied to me." I caught myself. "That's not true, I guess. I didn't ask her about her love life. Just about his."

"What would you expect her to do?" Linda asked. "Give you a list of all the guys she's slept with?"

"Good point, except she's the one who brought it up. She was about to do exactly that, I think, or something like it. I may have made a mistake by cutting her off."

"Maybe Abby just needs somebody to talk to," Linda added. "Or maybe Jeff and Abby have one of those marriages that thrive on conflict? It can be that way with two strong-willed people."

"That could be," I agreed. "I've known a few. Do you think that Abby and Jimmy Hopper had anything going on?"

"I don't know," Linda said. "I wouldn't be surprised, but it *is* possible for women to have men friends without sex involved. It's possible to be friends and have sex, too. It's even possible to have sex and not be friends. Now that I think about it, I'd guess that the answer is no, but that's just my gut feeling. I didn't know Jimmy well at all."

"You know, if Jeff called Abby a fucking slut, I wonder what he calls all the married women he had affairs with."

"Jeff doesn't think that way," Linda said. "You know that. If he does it, then it must be all right. When his wife does it, assuming that she *is* doing it, it's a crime against humanity, not to mention his ego. Remember Jeff's temper, too. When he gets fired up he says all kinds of things. When he called her that it does not necessarily mean that she is, in fact, fucking somebody else. Or maybe she isn't and he just thinks she is?"

Linda eased back in her chair. She hadn't finished her veal, but most of the women I knew never finished a meal. When Dina and I went out to eat, I usually ate one and a half dinners.

"There are a couple of other things," she said.

"Like what?"

"I don't know if Jeff knows who it is, or who he thinks it is. There may be more than one for all I know. But this other thing is something different than what's she's doing, or who she's doing it with. They refer to it, but it's always "it." They talk about it like it's in the future. One time I heard Jeff tell her, 'It's not gonna happen. I don't care what we have to do, it's not gonna happen.' Something like that."

"Have any thoughts on when this mysterious 'it' might happen?" I asked. "Days? Weeks? Months? Years?"

"Not real soon, I'd say. Not tomorrow or next week, but soon enough that Jeff can see it coming. He hates it, too. He just loathes it. His voice changes when he talks about it. It's as if he can barely deal with the thought."

"How long has all this been going on?" I asked.

"The 'it' part not long," she said. "A few weeks. The rest longer. Months, I'd guess."

We talked a little longer, but Linda couldn't add any more to what she'd already told me. I motioned for the check, produced a credit card, and signed the bill.

We walked outside. It was cooler now and the marina was ablaze with light and activity, most of it from the restaurants that lined the marina. Walking through there on a busy night was like running the gauntlet. Every establishment had somebody outside to try and lure you in with the best food and the cheapest prices in town. Cabo San Lucas had to have more restaurants per capita than any place on earth.

"Want me to take you back to wherever it is you're staying?" I asked.

"That's okay. I'll get another taxi. I'm staying in a company condo not far from here."

I waited with her while the taxi pulled up.

"Did any of this help?" she asked.

"Everything helps," I said. "Sometimes you don't know how until later when things start coming together. I appreciate it though. I'll be calling you again."

The beginnings of a grin crinkled around her eyes.

"When you say you'll call me again, does that mean you want me to spy on my boss?" she asked.

"I wouldn't say 'spy.' Just be extraordinarily attentive and aware and then tell me every little thing."

She stepped close and gave me a peck on the cheek.

"It was nice to see you again, Ethan," she said.

Her taxi arrived, the usual van, and we turned to go our separate ways.

Linda stopped in mid-turn. "Oh, yeah, I almost forgot. This doesn't have anything to do with what we talked about, but I know you've seen Mort a couple of times recently. Did he tell you that he's getting a divorce?"

"What!" I couldn't have been more surprised if she told me that Mort Bergman had a rap CD coming out.

"Jane's suing for divorce, Mort's not contesting, and everybody is agog."

"Good God! I bet they are. Why?"

"Who knows?" she said. "Maybe she was bored to death. He's not exactly Mister Excitement."

"And she's not exactly Mrs. Excitement. I always thought they were a perfect match."

"Everybody did," she said. "But I guess they weren't so perfect after all."

CHAPTER 17

I DROVE BACK THE HOUSE, parked the car, went inside, made myself a vodka and tonic, went out back to the darkness of the patio and flopped down in a chaise lounge.

It was too dark to see the ocean but I could hear the waves crashing on the shore with a boom that seemed to vibrate the ground. With the lights out, the sky seemed full of stars with a nice warm breeze to blow them around

I knew more than I did before I talked to Linda. That was good. But I wasn't sure how much of it had anything to do with the case I was working on. That was bad, or at least not good.

What did I have so far?

I knew that somebody was threatening Jeff and Abby LaForge.

I knew that they were watching, too, but not full time unless there was more than one of them.

I knew that somebody had killed Jimmy Hopper. That could be a coincidence, but I was sure that it wasn't.

I knew that somebody paid three meatheads to beat

me up, but I didn't know why. I still was offended that it came so cheap.

I was pretty sure Abby was screwing around. I seemed to be proof of that, unless I was a singular – and no doubt wonderful - experience, which was a flattering, if unlikely, thought.

From what Linda said, I was pretty sure Jeff knew about it, assuming there really was somebody else other than me.

I knew that Jeff probably wasn't screwing around, or if he was Linda didn't know about it and his wife, who seemed eager to tell me about everything, didn't mention it.

I knew that Abby and Jeff argued a lot.

I knew that it was getting worse.

I knew that something was going to happen, but I didn't know what. Whatever it was Jeff didn't like it. On the other hand, it wasn't necessarily a sure thing. According to Linda, Jeff talked about it like it was something that could be stopped, or something done about it.

I knew that Mort Bergman was getting a divorce. While that might be the shock of the century, for my purposes who the hell cared?

There was one last thing.

The three meatheads said they were supposed to break my leg or arm; something that showed. That meant whoever hired them had to be around to see it.

Which meant somebody was eyeballing me, too.

CHAPTER 18

ACCORDING to Cruickshank's Official Private Eye Rules, when in doubt, do something.

I decided to tail Jeff LaForge. If he was being watched, at least some of the time, maybe I could catch the watcher in the act? I'd stick with Cabo San Lucas because that's where I was, that's where LaForge spent a lot of his time these days, and Tom Hauser probably had his end of things covered.

But I didn't want LaForge to know what I was doing. When someone knows they're being followed, it changes their behavior. The urge to look around and see if they can spot the person who's following them is almost irresistible and might tip somebody else. Too, they may not do things they normally do, or go to places they normally go, because it could be embarrassing. If LaForge was a member of the Cabo Cross Dressers Club, he probably wouldn't attend the weekly meeting if he knew I was tailing him.

It would be easier to track him if I had a good idea of where he was supposed to be at any given time. I called Linda Giordano and asked if she could give me his schedule of appointments.

"No problem," she said.

"Okay, just put it in an envelope and I'll come by and get it. Didn't you say your boss is in Denver?"

"Yeah, but he changed his plans and he's now coming back this afternoon," she said. "There's a big do here tonight and he's going."

"Abby, too."

"I think so."

"By the way," I said, "don't tell Jeff."

"Okey dokey," she said. "Do you suppose this could get me fired?"

"I doubt it," I said. "Jeff *did* employ me and this *is* part of my investigation. Just to be sure, I won't tell him."

I drove over to LaForge's gigantic facility west of town. From the outside, it looked like a massive warehouse, which is more or less what it was; LaForge's North American distribution and call center. As I understood it, if this one worked out it would be the first of many.

The security was the same as it was up north. The guy at the desk handed me a visitor's badge.

"Haga a y llevelo," he said, telling me in what I think was supposed to be a threatening manner to wear it.

"Si," I said as I walked away and slipped it into my pocket.

As I made my way to the corporate offices - after stopping twice to ask directions - I knew that my behavior was juvenile. But so what? Sometimes I enjoyed being juvenile. Growing up is overrated. The next time I might go, "Nyah! Nyah! Nyah!" and stick out my tongue.

I finally found Linda Giordano's desk. She handed me the envelope with LaForge's schedule.

"Thanks, kiddo," I said. "I enjoyed dinner."

"Me, too," she said. "By the way, Mort's here. He's going to the thing tonight, too."

She told me how to get to Bergman's office. The door

was open and he was sitting behind his desk. He had his head in his hands and his eyes were down as if he was reading something laid flat on his desk, except that nothing was there.

I rapped on the door frame. "Mort?" I said.

He raised his head. I never thought of him as a particularly handsome man, but today he seemed deflated, as if everything about him sagged a little.

"Look, it's none of my business, but I heard about you and Jane," I said. "If there's anything I can do …."

It was as if a furnace door suddenly opened and I could see the white-hot flames raging inside. Bergman's face tightened and the bones under the flesh seemed more prominent. Somehow the atmosphere in the room changed, too, as he emanated a feeling of rage that was like a force pressing against me. It was such a shocking transformation that I had the urge to step back to protect myself.

The door closed just as suddenly as it opened and the Mort Bergman I knew was sitting at his desk.

"I appreciate it, Ethan, but there's nothing you can do," he said quietly. "There's nothing anybody can do. It's just one of life's things"

"Okay," I said. "Just wanted you to know."

I passed the guard on the way out, flipped the visitor's badge on his desk with as much disdain as I could summon, and walked out to the Mustang.

I opened the door, got in and sat for a moment with the door open in the afternoon heat. What I'd seen on Bergman's face took my breath away. I didn't understand what that phrase meant until this minute. I felt sorry for him, but now I wondered about him, too.

CHAPTER 19

ACCORDING TO LINDA GIORDANO, tonight's bash was to celebrate the official opening of LaForge's facility in Cabo, although it had actually been open for a while. All kinds of officials would be there, national down to local, and I decided that I would be there, too.

I usually hated this kind of thing. Dina's public relations business meant that she attended a lot of them, which meant that I did, too. Every time I went to one, I swore that it was my last, which it was until the next time she talked me into attending one.

Even worse, Linda Giordano promised that there would be a strolling mariachi band, which was almost enough to make me give up the detecting business because I hated mariachi music, though I did kind of like the outfits.

The shindig was supposed to start at eight but I got there at seven thirty because I wanted to see people arriving. I didn't know what I was looking for, but I hoped that I'd know it when I saw it. The festivities were set up in the big inner courtyard, where the modern glass and granite design showed off a lot better than the building's bland stucco-on-cinder-block exterior. The contrast was almost shocking. It seemed like an entirely different place.

After the opening ceremony and dedication, from what Linda Giordano told me the rest of the night would be devoted to the party, with everyone standing around with a drink in one hand, something edible in the other, and an insincere smile on their beamers. Mariachi music would play; there would be laughter and merriment. One and all would have a good time. Or else.

She also revealed that LaForge didn't intend to come at first, excusing himself with a vague explanation of unavoidable business elsewhere, and was content to leave Bergman in charge. When he realized how many dignitaries would be there, from the President of Mexico on down, LaForge decided that only he could handle it, with his beautiful wife at his side, of course. For all he cared, Mort Bergman, his faithful number two for many years, could go pound sand.

I was the epitome of the dashing private detective in a teal jacket, black shirt, black trousers and black tasseled loafers. Topping off my fabulous *ensemble*, the accessories included a lovely black leather shoulder holster, accented by a Smith & Wesson Centennial with a walnut grip. Being hammerless, the Centennial is ideal for a concealed carry. That was why I wore the jacket. I was tired of the ankle rig and if I had to arm myself quickly, the shoulder holster was easier. I wore no tie because the jacket already made me feel overdressed. This was Cabo, after all. I'd never even seen a tie here. Fashion is my life.

With hundreds of people expected to attend, LaForge provided valet parking. I handed off the Mustang to a little guy whose legs didn't look long enough to reach the gas pedal and walked through the building to the court-yard, ignoring a glare from the same guard I met earlier, who no doubt remembered my rank disobedience and vowed that he would have his vengeance one day.

By eight thirty at least five hundred people were gathered in front of a temporary elevated stage at one end of the courtyard. The President of Mexico, a handsome silver-haired man who, by reputation, never met a payoff he didn't like, said a few words in his distinguished way and quickly left with his phalanx of security men to go elsewhere and do whatever it is that presidents do.

Some other high-ranking politico, a fat character with a bad comb over, took his place at the podium and began babbling the usual baloney, with a lineup of dignitaries seated behind him on a row of metal folding chairs. I could see that this was going to be a long night. No matter what country, I tended to regard politics like a sport that didn't interest me, like, say, soccer or NASCAR racing. Somebody wins, somebody loses, and it never seems to matter. Occasionally I ran into a politician I admired, but not often enough to keep me interested.

With her business, of necessity Dina had known a lot more of these people than I did, including what they did for a living, their hobbies, pets, what kind of cars they drove, their spouses' names, the names of their children, and how the little darlings were doing in school. As I circulated, all the while keeping an eye on LaForge, I dealt with a lot of condolence and "I'm so sorry" from people who knew her.

I also ran into Garcia, who I'd called in to keep an eye on Abby.

"How's it going?" I asked.

"So far, I've learned how to climb a palm tree and pull down dead palm fronds," he said. "I like this duty better."

"You never knew that undercover work could be that glamorous, did you?" I said.

"I suppose I now have – how do you say it? - *habili-dades transferibles.*"

"Transferable skills," I laughed. "Yeah, I guess that's one way to look at it. How are things at *casa* LaForge?"

"They fight," he said. "Often. Then they make up with sex. You would be surprised what you can hear, and sometimes see, from up in a palm tree."

I didn't want that image to take up permanent residence in my head, so I asked, "Are you armed?"

Garcia nodded. "The Glock."

"Okay, keep moving around, but stay within reasonable distance of Abby. Give me the high sign if you see anything suspicious. And tomorrow, try not to fall out of a palm tree while you're gaping."

Once the speeches mercifully came to and end, the crowd gathered around the many portable bars scattered throughout the courtyard, desperate to get a drink, while the caterer's staff circulated bearing trays loaded with finger food.

I wandered over to one of the bars. I was pretty sure that LaForge wouldn't dare run a no-host bar for this occasion. The discovery that I was right renewed my faith in large grasping business institutions.

In my usual lunatic Spanglish, I asked, "What do you have in the way of a *cerveza para un hombre sediento y desperado*?" I asked, hitting the thirsty and desperate man part hard.

The bartender looked like he wasn't old enough to do what he was doing. His snazzy bartender's outfit consisted of a paisley vest, a black clip-on bow tie, a short-sleeved white shirt and dark pants. He stepped to one side and gestured to the array of beer on the counter behind him. I picked Bohemia, not bothering with a glass.

He reached down behind the bar and produced a bottle. He unscrewed the top and offered me a napkin. I shook my head and he handed me the bottle. I stuffed a buck into his tip jar, stepped away and let the next man take my place. Judging by the length of the line, it was a thirsty crowd. Speeches have that effect.

Beer in hand, I strolled along the perimeter of the party, keeping LaForge in sight, hoping to find something edible. I was about half way around the perimeter when I spotted the shrimp. I was able to work it out so that I could watch LaForge from fairly close and eat shrimp at the same time. I didn't think that anyone would be foolish enough to make a move on him with so many people around, but I wanted to see if anyone else was watching him.

I had to admit that Jeff and Abby made a fine looking couple. He wore black loafers, black trousers, and a white jacket over a silver shirt. She wore eye-catching red, a dress that somehow managed to seem reasonably modest while at the same time showing off her figure.

After a few minutes I decided to leave some shrimp for everybody else. I tossed my empty beer bottle into a green plastic trash container, wiped off my hands with a napkin, and began working my way through the crowd in the LaForges' direction. I didn't have anything in mind. I just didn't have anything else to do.

I was about forty feet away when a heavy-set dark-haired woman carrying a paper plate of food in one hand and a plastic glass with white wine in the other slipped on a wet spot about ten feet in front of me. She was wearing white high heels and when her feet began to slide out from under her she couldn't regain her balance because her hands were full.

A young flashy looking guy with dark eyes, hollow cheeks and shiny black hair combed straight back was on her opposite side. She fell against him in the crowd and he had to catch her to keep from going down himself.

When he put his arms out his jacket opened and I saw a shoulder holster with weapon in it.

He caught her with a hand under each arm as her food and wine sprayed all over the floor. She probably outweighed him by at least forty pounds and he had to strain to keep from going down himself. With his help, she finally regained her balance and began blubbering apologies to everyone between here and Tierra del Fuego. Slick hair gave her a venomous glare and backed away. I turned my back and moved in the other direction to put some bodies between us. I didn't want him to get a good look at me. By the time I turned back, he'd moved on.

Maybe there was a good reason for this guy to be carrying a gun. I was carrying one myself, but I knew why.

It wasn't hard to track him. I tried to stay at a distance so that he couldn't easily pick me out of the crowd, but still close enough that if he tried anything I could stop him. I didn't expect him to shoot my client in a courtyard crowded with hundreds of people, but stranger things have happened. He didn't seem to be watching the LaForges. He didn't seem to be doing anything at all, the very picture of youthful nonchalance. But that didn't mean anything. I was trying hard not to seem to be watching him, too.

After a few minutes, Linda Giordano saw me, graced me with a smile, and wondered over. She looked good in a knee-length black cocktail dress; as good as Abby, in fact, and that was no small achievement.

Before she could say anything, I leaned over and whispered in her ear, "Keep smiling and laughing like I'm the wittiest man alive. I'm watching somebody and you're good cover."

She turned her face up to me and laughed.

"How's that?" she asked, still smiling.

"Good. He keeps moving around so it's best you not stay with me too long."

She laughed again because I am such a clever fellow and kissed me on the cheek.

"Be careful," she whispered.

We spent the next thirty minutes in a kind of bizarre dance. Slick hair led and I followed without seeming to. Between us, we managed to cover most of the room. I talked to several people I knew, always watching him out of the corner of my eye while trying to act like I'd never had a better time in my life. He didn't seem to know anyone, or if he did he didn't talk to them. He didn't drink. He didn't eat. He was just there.

The party was thinning out and it was getting harder to watch him without being obvious about it. I had to come up with a plan pretty soon. It wouldn't do for the two of us to be the only people left in the room. I thought about saying something to Garcia, but while I didn't think the guy had spotted me watching him, I wasn't sure. I didn't want to spook him by seeming to call in reinforcements. Maybe I was being paranoid, but this looked like it might be a break and I didn't want to screw it up.

I casually walked up to LaForge. Standing at his side, I interrupted a conversation and whispered in his ear, "Act like I'm making cocktail party chat. I need you and Abby to leave in a couple of minutes. I think you're being followed and I want to see what he does when you go."

He smiled and slapped me on the shoulder. In a too-loud voice, he said, "Ethan, it's good to see you." Not being in on what was going on, Abby stared at her husband as if he'd gone stark raving mad. We made phony small talk for a minute, and I moved on. After a few minutes, I saw Jeff whisper in Abby's ear. She nodded. They said their goodbyes and headed toward the exit.

It was a pretty safe bet that slick hair got here in a car. That meant he either used the valet parking or left his car somewhere outside. I waited to see what he'd do now that the LaForges were leaving. If he was interested in them, he'd leave, too. If he parked somewhere out on the street I'd have a problem trying to follow him because I couldn't recover my car from the valet fast enough.

To my surprise, he didn't do anything. He kept hanging around like he was determined to eat the last mini-taco on the last plate, except that he didn't eat anything. Maybe he was security for somebody at the party? Maybe he just liked to carry a gun? Maybe he just liked to carry a gun at parties? Maybe I was losing my mind?

By now there couldn't have been more than a hundred people left. The courtyard was so big it seemed even fewer than that. Time was running out. It was possible that he'd seen me watching him and let the LaForges go because he didn't want to tip his hand.

What if I left? What would he do then?

I strolled back to Linda Giordano, who was deep in conversation with two young women who looked like they could be sisters. If I read her body language right, she'd never been more bored in her life.

I smiled my killer smile at the young ladies, offered many pardons, took Linda by the elbow and stepped away.

Gesturing like I was giving directions, I said, "I'm going outside. If that guy with the slick hair standing beside the table by the wall on your left leaves by another way, hurry out and get me. I'll be right outside the front entrance. If he comes out after me I'm going to try to follow him."

She winked and strolled away. Once I got outside I ran to the other side of the street and hid around the corner of a dumpy looking one-story building. About five seconds later, my boy walked out. He stopped at the corner and looked around like he'd lost something. Apparently he didn't find it. In a fast walk, he headed down the street.

I waited for a moment to let him get well ahead and sprinted over to the other side of the street. He walked another block and turned right. I ran across the street and carefully peered around the corner. He'd just started a British racing green Mazda Miata parked about twenty feet down from the corner. I got out my Mont Blanc, wrote the license number on the little notebook I always carried with me, and watched him drive away.

I walked back to what remained of the party. Linda was still there, sipping a glass of white wine and making conversation with the same two women. This time she looked so bored that suicide might be a real possibility.

"Hi," I said.

"Well, hello again," she said, smiling her relief.

This time she introduced me to the two women. I didn't catch their names because I wasn't really listening.

"Everything all right?" she asked.

"Couldn't be better," I replied. "Just wanted to let you know that I think I'll take off."

"Want me to come with you?"

"That's okay. I've got some things to take care of."

With a nod at the two young ladies, I went back outside, handed my ticket to the valet, recovered my car, and drove home.

On the way, I wondered what Linda Giordano meant when she asked if I wanted her to come with me.

CHAPTER 20

VALENCIA HADN'T ATTENDED the opening ceremony. He hated that kind of thing even more than I did, although I was sure that he had some men in the crowd.

I called him on his cell and asked him to run a license number. I had no idea where he was when I called but ten minutes later he called back to say that the green Miata was registered to somebody named Adnan Gallegos. The address was an apartment within a mile of where we were last night.

"Is there anything I should know?" he asked.

"As soon as I know something, you'll know something," I lied.

I didn't want to blunder around in the dark in an unfamiliar area so I wanted until morning before I clipped the address to the visor of the Mustang and took off. The address was in an area that consisted of a small oasis of shabby apartment buildings in a desert of run-down commercial, mostly a bunch of small shops that catered to the locals and looked like they were barely making it, if they were making it at all. The street had been paved about a hundred years ago and there were great cracks running from curb to curb that served as natural speed bumps. The whole setting looked like a small pustule of residential blight in the middle of much larger commercial blight. What greenery existed was entirely devoted to weeds.

The two-story apartment building where Gallegos lived was rectangular, with the narrow ends of the building facing the street and alley behind it. It had eight apartments, four upstairs and four downstairs. Gallegos' address was upstairs, one from the back as I faced the building from the front.

There was a small parking area in back. The green Miata wasn't in it. I drove around the neighborhood on the streets and through the alleys and didn't see the Miata anywhere. It looked like he wasn't home.

I parked down the street and called Garcia. I wanted whatever information I could get on this guy, but I didn't want to get Valencia involved, at least not yet. Garcia was young, but he had experience and might have access to sources that an official like Valencia didn't.

"You're not up a tree, or anything are you?" I asked.

"If I was, I wouldn't be answering the telephone. I am not as *loco* as I look."

"You ever run across somebody named Adnan Gallegos; skinny, dark hair slicked back, drives a green Miata? Lives here in Cabo."

"No, but let me make a few calls," he said, the relief at getting off gardening detail again, if only for a short time, clear in his voice. "Since you're asking *me* I assume that you don't want my uncle to know. How soon do you need it?"

"I don't what him to know, at least not yet, and quick as you can."

A less than a half hour, Garcia called back.

"I have what you wanted," he said.

"Tell me about him."

"He is - how do you put it? - a professional fuck up. He thinks that he's tough and connected but he's just a fool who works for people many levels down from people who really are tough and connected. They don't want to be bothered with the kind of *mierda* somebody like Gallegos does for them. He could live to be a hundred and never be more than what he is right now."

"He doesn't exactly sound like public enemy number one," I said.

"Or number nine ninety nine," Garcia said. "Can I help?"

I told him about spotting the guy at the party.

"I don't know if he speaks English," Garcia said. "Would you like me to talk to him?"

"Assuming he knows anything, to get what we want might take more than conversation," I said.

"I could talk to him very hard."

I thought about it. Garcia's offer was tempting. It might save a lot of time and trouble.

"Not yet," I said. "I don't even know if he has anything to do with what we're working on. Based on what you found out, would he shoot anybody?"

"I don't think he has the *cojones*," Garcia said. "Even if he tried, he'd probably shoot himself in the foot."

"Let me rephrase the question," I said. "Would anyone be likely to employ him to shoot somebody?"

"Not if they knew what they were doing," he said. "Somebody who didn't know better might be fooled by his line of *mierda*. To a regular person, he probably seems like he's *muy malo*. To a real hard ass, he might as well be Frida Kahlo."

"Okay, thanks."

"Let me know if I can help," he said.

I sat in the car and thought about what Garcia told me and how it might fit in with what I thought that I knew. I had the window down and even this far inland there was a light breeze. Should I break into the apartment to see if I could find anything? I couldn't see how it would hurt. At least it was something to do. I was supposed to be following LaForge, but this was more promising.

I dressed this morning with just such a possibility in mind; jeans, a dark blue pullover shirt, and a pair of brown ankle-high Rockports with soft soles. Anyone who saw me might take me for a workman or an inspector of some kind. Most Mexicans don't like to confront authority. In fact, they go out of their way to avoid it. I didn't blame them. Over the course of Mexican history, authority was rarely kind. I lifted my gun from the glove compartment. I got out of the car, put the weapon in my waistband and pulled my shirt tail out to hide it, careful to face the car so no one could see me do it. I opened the trunk and got a gym bag with the necessary tools. I walked down the street, turned right at the corner, turned left into the alley in back of the apartment, and went up the rusting metal stairs to the second floor. I stopped outside the door and looked around. I was too far back to be seen from the street and there was no one in the alley.

I knocked on the door and no one answered. I knocked again, still nothing. After that, it didn't take long. The lock was cheap and the door was even cheaper. I didn't have to damage the lock to get in. I was taking a chance that Gallegos wouldn't come home while I was in his apartment, or that he didn't have a girlfriend or roommate inside who ignored my knock. I didn't think that either one was likely. Besides, I didn't need much time. Even if he came home, based on what Garcia said, the idea of getting caught did not terrify me.

I could tell no one was there the minute I opened the door. There's a peculiar stillness to an empty place that doesn't feel like anything else.

I walked through to get the feel of it. The apartment was pretty much what it seemed to be from the outside: small, cheap and badly furnished with one bedroom. It was more or less square. The entrance opened to a combination living and dining room, although there was no dining table. Just beyond it was a small kitchen. The bathroom and bedroom were to the right down a short hallway.

The bed was unmade and sink was piled high with dirty dishes. A search of the wastebasket under the sink revealed nothing except trash. There were no books or newspapers anywhere in the apartment. Three porn magazines were in a pile on the floor by the side of a recliner that had stuffing coming out of a rips in the arms. From what I saw hanging in his closet, Gallegos had three changes of clothes and they all hurt my eyes.

I went through the bedroom dresser and discovered that Gallegos favored briefs, and very brief they were, too. He smoked grass. I found a couple of ounces in a baggie hidden underneath his socks, next to a forty five Colt with a pearl handled grip. How tacky. I remembered a line from "Patton" about how only a pimp from a cheap New Orleans whorehouse would carry a gun with a pearl handled grip. Patton himself preferred ivory. It wasn't a forty five I saw last night, so now I knew that he was the proud owner of at least two weapons. There didn't seem to be any spare ammunition around. Obviously, the man was a minimalist. There was nothing under the bed but dust.

A search of the bathroom revealed that, among other things, Gallegos used Brut cologne. I was surprised that they still sold Brut. When I was about seventeen I thought it was cool, but I hadn't been seventeen in a long time.

There was a small desk in the bedroom with the wood

veneer peeling off and a laptop computer on a stand next to it. After rummaging through the desk and finding nothing, I turned on the computer and checked out the documents as best I could. A personal computer could be a treasure trove of information and almost everybody had one. The only document that looked interesting was a list of names, addresses, and telephone numbers, along with a few comments after four or five of the names. Without taking the time to read it, I made a printout. I could translate the Spanish later.

The wastebasket next to the desk was so full that it overflowed. Most of the trash was discarded mail, most of it not even opened. I dumped the contents on the floor and went through everything piece by piece, refilling the wastebasket as I went.

I was almost through with trash patrol when I found a crumpled white envelope with Jeff LaForge's business address in Mexico on the return address spot in the upper left corner. Gallegos's name and address were written across the front in blue ink. That meant it wasn't official. Official was never hand written. This was an envelope someone used for personal communication. I held the envelope in my hand and stared at it. Did I have an actual clue here? This was no time to savor the moment. I folded the envelope in half and put it in my hip pocket. I got to my feet and walked through the apartment to make sure that I'd left everything exactly as I found it.

Satisfied that Gallegos wouldn't know anyone had broken into his dump, I picked up my gym bag, closed the door and walked down the metal stairs to the parking area leading to the alley.

I had to fight my instinct to hurry. People remember a man in a hurry. They probably wouldn't remember someone who looked like he belonged and knew what he was doing.

I walked up the alley, turned, walked a half block, turned again walked another half block and got to my car. I put the gym bag back in the trunk, started the Mustang and drove away.

The envelope felt like it was burning a hole in my pocket. I was sweating a little, too. It wasn't from the heat.

CHAPTER 21

BACK AT THE HOUSE, I smoothed out the envelope on my desk and stared at it, but it refused to talk.

If it could talk, what would it say? There were a hundred reasons why Adnan Gallegos might have an envelope from LaForge's company, but ninety nine of them didn't do me any good. There was a link somewhere. It might mean absolutely nothing, but I had to find out what it was. This was a lot more promising than anything I'd found so far.

I looked at the list that I'd printed out from his computer. There were about thirty names and they weren't organized in alphabetical order, or any other way I could figure out. The few comments were so cryptic that they made no sense, except presumably to Gallegos. I didn't recognize anybody on the list except me.

Except me? I looked at it again. There I was, the last one on page two; name and home address. My, my, wasn't that interesting? Two clues in an hour, or so. It was enough to make a detective feel lightheaded.

I fired up the computer and began to learn what I could about Adnan Gallegos.

There wasn't much, a lot of it was in Spanish, and

although I labored over the translation I was sure that I got the gist of it; the man just barely existed. Gallegos was twenty five years old, five feet, eight inches tall and weighed a hundred and thirty pounds. He was born in a small town on the mainland, one that I'd never heard of. His parents were deceased. He had no brothers or sisters. He'd never been married. He'd been arrested several times, but only went to court twice. One was a drug case. The other was battery. Both times the charges were nego-tiated down to nothing. There was no record of employ-ment in the last three years and no record of taxes paid in that time. Whatever he did, he did it for cash. Judging by his apartment, not very much cash either. His skills, if he had any, were not highly valued. His last known job was at Galaxy Imports. I recognized the name. It was a front to smuggle illegal Mexican and Asian aliens into the United States. It should have been shut down a long time ago, but mine not to reason why. For all I knew, Galaxy Imports was a hotbed of undercover agents. They were probably all busy keeping an eye on each other. Appar-ently, he did speak English, but not fluently.

After two hours, satisfied that there was nowhere else to look and nothing more to find out, I pushed myself away from the computer.

I leaned back in my chair and put my feet on the desk. My research hadn't told me much, and nothing at all that was useful. What little I'd learned didn't even give me anyone to talk to. He had no parents, no siblings, no wife, and no obvious employer. There was no sign of compan-ionship in his apartment, male or female, and no pets, not even a goldfish. There was nothing at all. Garcia told me more in two minutes than the computer coughed up in two hours. So much for twenty first century technology.

But I knew his type. I ran into it everywhere. People like Gallegos lived on the margin and never escaped.

They lived and they died and nobody cared. He was a bottom feeder on the best day he ever had. Unless he was given to grave introspection he probably didn't realize it either. Guys like him usually didn't go in for introspection, grave or otherwise. It's too depressing and demands too much brainpower.

But he had my name and address. Why? He was in communication with someone from LaForge's company. Why? He was at the party. Why?

Seeking inspiration, I swiveled in my chair and looked out the window. It was another beautiful sun-filled afternoon. In other words, it was a good day to be out on the beach or on the ocean.

Just for the hell of it, I took my binoculars out of the bottom desk drawer to see what I could see. I focused just in time to see a nicely built blond in a thong and a top that wouldn't make a decent eye patch climb out of the water into an expensive boat about a hundred yards off short and casually towel herself off. From a distance, most of her parts looked real, but not, alas, all of them. Real or artificial, such a sight is always encouraging. It has a way of renewing a man's faith in something or other. I took it as a good omen, like the first robin of spring only a lot better.

It didn't have anything to do with my case, but good omens are where you find them.

CHAPTER 22

I WAS SUPPOSED to meet LaForge the next morning. I wanted to find out if he'd ever heard of Gallegos. I also wanted to check with LaForge's personnel department to see if Gallegos had any work history there. It hadn't shown up on the computer, but the Internet wasn't infallible. It just thought it was.

As I left the house and approached the highway leading to Cabo San Lucas, I glanced in my rear view mirror and beheld a green Miata. I wouldn't have believed it unless I saw it myself, and it reinforced my conclusion that Gallegos was a major league bonehead. For one thing, he drove the wrong car for a successful tail. There's more than one British racing green Miata in the world, but there aren't that many either, certainly not in Cabo San Lucas. It's too easy to pick out. True, when it comes to concealment my Mustang wasn't exactly ideal either. That's why I rented a car whenever I did a tail, something boring and anonymous. Apparently that never occurred to Gallegos. From what I saw last night, he couldn't afford it anyway.

Many years ago there was a TV series named "Magnum, P.I." The hero was a private detective who used to tail people in a bright red Ferrari, which is only a little less conspicuous than an aircraft carrier. Worse than that, Magnum usually followed so closely that if the subject looked in the rear view mirror he could have counted the hairs in the detective's mustache. It looked like Gallegos learned everything he knew from watching old "Magnum" reruns. At least he didn't use tips from "77 Sunset Strip."

Now I had to figure out what to do with the unexpected opportunity. I decided to go ahead and drive to LaForge's office. Knowing the turf made it easier to put together a plan.

I made it as easy for Gallegos as possible. For about ten minutes I didn't as much as change lanes, which allowed him to keep his distance. Once we got into Cabo, he immediately tightened the tail "Magnum" style. He didn't have to be as close as he was, but it looked like he didn't know any better. It was always possible he didn't care if I spotted him, but I didn't think that was very likely. He probably thought that he was doing one hell of a job.

I parked in a visitor's spot in the parking lot. Gallegos would have to park where he could keep an eye both on my car and the building's entrance in case I left with someone else. His only option was to park across the street, probably down the block near a corner so he wouldn't get sandwiched between two cars.

I walked into the lobby. The guard yelled that I should stop in the name of the law, or something. I ignored him. I ran downstairs, hustled through what looked like the shipping department, and came out of the back of the building at the loading dock. I jumped off the dock, turned left, and jogged along the alley behind a cinder-block wall that separated the alley from the parking lot. The wall was an important part of my plan because it kept Gallegos from spotting me. I turned left at the end of the block, jogged another short block and stopped when I came to the street in front of the building.

I peeked around the wall and there he was, parked right where I thought he'd be. He was sitting in his car on the other side of the street. The day was already warm and getting warmer. The Miata's convertible top was up but the driver's side window was down and the door was slightly ajar for air circulation. Gallegos had one arm hanging outside the door as he waited for me to reappear so he could follow me some more.

I walked in the opposite direction to put some distance between us before crossing to his side of the street. I approached the Miata from the passenger side, sticking to what should be Gallegos's blind spot if he looked in the mirror. I felt pretty safe. His attention would be on the entrance and parking lot. He wouldn't be expecting anything from in back. If he was as dumb as I thought, I wouldn't be surprised if he'd fallen asleep.

As I got closer, I took my gun out and held it down at my side. I opened the Miata's passenger door with my left hand, climbed in and jammed my gun against the side of his face.

"*Buenos dias*," I said.

He tried to swing open his door and get out, but a Miata isn't built for a quick exit. I grabbed his shirt collar and yanked him back inside, this time pressing the gun against his thigh.

"If you move again I'm going to shoot you in the leg," I said. "As skinny as you are it'll probably shatter the bone and they'll have to amputate. On the other hand, you'll have great parking for the rest of your life. Is it worth it?"

I didn't know if he had enough English to appreciate my little joke, but it amused the hell out of me.

Gallegos wasn't wearing a jacket, so there was no shoulder holster this time. He wore a long-sleeved black and white striped polyester shirt with the tail out, one of the limited wardrobe choices that I remembered when I broke into his place. I ran my left hand around his belt line. Nothing there.

"Where is it?" I asked.

"*E-e-entre los asientos*," he stammered.

I looked down. The pearl-handled forty five was jammed between the driver and passenger seats. Keeping my gun on his thigh, I picked up the forty five with my left hand and put it on the floor near my feet. The maneuver was awkward, but I managed.

I had to make sure he didn't have anything else tucked away.

"*Levante las piernas de pantalones, una pierna a la vez*," I said.

There were times when my clumsy way with the language was a real handicap, like now. I thought that I got it right, but then again I might have asked him to change the oil in my car. Imagine the relief I felt when he looked at me as if I were some kind of pervert who wanted to stare at his legs.

"Just do it." I pressed my gun a little deeper into his thigh to reinforce the order.

He lifted one pants leg, then the other. There was no ankle holster and no knife.

"Okay," I said. "Let's talk. English?"

He nodded.

"What are you doing here?"

He shrugged. "I am meeting someone."

I hit him in the ear with my left fist. Getting hit in the ear hurts and he yelped, raising a hand to the side of his head.

"That was the wrong answer," I said. "Put your hand down."

There were tears in his eyes. "*Que duelen!*"

"It was supposed to hurt, stupid. Now tell me, what are you doing?"

"I meet ..."

Before he could finish I cracked him across the bridge of the nose with my gun. Getting hit in the nose hurts even worse than getting hit in the ear. He yelped again, put his head down and both hands went to his face to cup his nose.

I jabbed him in the ribs with my gun. "Put your hands down and keep looking forward!"

Getting bashed in the nose made his eyes water. It would have made anybody's eyes water, but he was in no condition to think about it. Sitting in his own car with tears running down his face while I beat on him from the passenger seat was humiliating, which was what I wanted. Gallegos thought he was a tough guy. He wasn't, but he was too dumb to know it. I had to prove it to him. I had to show him that I could do anything I wanted and there wasn't anything he could do about it.

"All right, let's try again," I said. "Why are you following me?"

"I not ...."

I backhanded him across the mouth with my left hand. Sitting in the car, I couldn't get my body into it, but it was still a pretty good shot. He made a pathetic little whimpering sound.

"I said keep your hands down!"

I jabbed him in the ribs with the barrel of my gun and was rewarded with another whimper.

"I can sit here and hit you all day," I said. "You'll get tired of it a long time before I do."

I thought he might start crying. It was mostly frustration and humiliation mixed with a little pain.

"All you have to do is answer the question. Why are you following me?"

This time he didn't say anything. It wasn't that he was brave. He was trying to hang on to what little self-respect he had left. The problem with thinking you're a tough guy is that sometimes you have to act like it. He wasn't up to the task.

With my left hand, I grabbed a fistful of hair at the back of his head and slammed his face into the Miata's steering wheel. The steering wheel was padded, but the padding didn't help much.

When he involuntarily reached for his face I jabbed him in the side with my gun again.

"Keep your hands down and keep looking forward!"

His nose was bleeding. He ran his tongue across his upper lip, tasting his own blood. He'd probably have a black eye, too.

"Why are you following me?"

I made a motion with my left hand and he flinched. There was nothing wrong with his peripheral vision.

"*Si, si.*" He was practically blubbering. "I get a call from a guy," he said. "He say he has job for me, for my services."

That didn't sound like a word Gallegos would use on his own.

"He said your 'services?'"

"*Si.*"

"Go ahead."

"He pay five hundred dollars a week to follow you. If it is not so many days I keep all the money. I tell him what you do, where you go, and who you talk."

"You work cheap," I said.

He didn't say anything. I didn't expect him to.

"Did you meet him?"

"No. He send me the first payment in advance, in business, uh, wrapping ..." He was struggling to find the word.

"Envelope?"

"Si," he nodded.

The one I found in the trash.

"How'd you report to him?"

"He say he call me at a same time every day. The first last night at eleven."

"When did you start?"

He was starting to get his bravado back. His shoulders had stiffened and his fists were clenched in his lap. When he didn't answer right away I hit him in the ear again. I was repeating myself. It happens when you get older. He didn't expect it and the surprise took all the starch out of him. He slumped in his seat and hunched his head between his shoulders like he was trying to shrink out of sight so I wouldn't hit him anymore.

"Day before yesterday," he mumbled, looking down at his lap. I was pretty sure he was crying.

"At the party here?" I asked, waving at the building with my gun hand.

"*Si.*"

"If you were following me, why did you leave before I did?"

Turning his head a fraction, he looked at me out of the corner of his eye.

"I think maybe you see me when that fat one fall down, so I wait a little and go."

"You moron, I made you on the day you were born."

I had no idea where that line came from, probably from an old movie. But I liked it. It was worth saving and using some other time, especially since Gallegos didn't understand what the hell I was talking about.

"Why is my name and address in your computer?"

That one surprised him. He probably understood English better than he could speak it. I had the same problem going the other way. He started to turn toward me, but stopped and jerked back when I made a motion with my left hand. It was like playing with Pavlov's dog.

"How you know?"

"I know everything about you and your worthless little life."

"A list I keep," he said. "Things I do."

"A client list," I said.

He just looked at me.

"Do you have the guy's number?"

He shook his head.

"When will he call next?"

"Tonight same time."

"Your place?"

Another nod.

I thought for a minute. I had an idea and I was looking for holes in it. When I didn't find any, I decided to go ahead.

"Here's what we're gonna do," I said, speaking slowly to be sure that he understood. "You've got two phones at your place. I will be there tonight for the call. I'll come at ten thirty. I'll tell you what to say when he calls and I'll listen when you say it. In the meantime, you're gonna pretend we never talked."

I had to repeat the instruction twice before he realized that he didn't like it.

"I can't …."

I grabbed him by the chin, jerked his head around so that he faced me and pressed my gun hard on his nose.

"Yes, you can," I said. "Do you know why?"

He shook his head in short little side-to-side motions. Between the gun and my grip on his chin, it wasn't easy. I wasn't sure if he was trying to say that he didn't know why or or begging me to stop.

"Because it'll really piss me off if you don't."

I let go of his chin and got out of the Miata, remembering to pick up his forty five. I put his gun in my waistband. The thing was so big there was barely room left in my pants for me. I crouched down so my head was even with the passenger window.

"Gallegos, I'll see you tonight at ten thirty. Now get the hell out of here before I change my mind and beat you to death. And don't try to run."

I stepped back from the car. He started the Miata and drove away, grinding the hell out of the transmission as he motored down the street.

The poor dunce was scared to death. I didn't blame him. I'd been pretty rough. If I was him, I'd be scared of me, too.

CHAPTER 23

I RAN to my car and called Garcia on the way.

"Stop whatever you're doing," I said. I gave him Gallegos' address and description, including his car. "Get over there as fast as you can and watch the guy we talked about yesterday. If he leaves town, and I think he probably will, make sure he's really gone and then call me."

I called LaForge to apologize for being late. He asked about what happened at the party. I told him it was a false alarm. I explained that I couldn't keep our appointment because I had a lead I wanted to follow. He wanted to know what it was and when I explained that I'd tell him later he got a little huffy. I huffed back.

I drove to Gallegos' apartment. As I expected, the Miata was there, parked in the lot in back. A short distance away, so was Garcia, who must have broken all kinds of speed records getting here. He saw me drive by, but didn't react in case someone was watching. Good man.

I parked a block away, out of sight of both Garcia and Gallegos' apartment. I waited for what seemed like a long time but really wasn't much more than an hour.

My cell phone rang. It was Garcia.

"He's gone, but I'm still following." Garcia explained that he watched Gallegos make several trips back and forth between the apartment and the Miata. He put two suitcases in the small space in back of the seats, crammed a few more things in the tiny trunk, and followed that up by laying his clothes on the passenger's seat. He didn't even bother to take the clothes off the hangers. After that, he came out with several cardboard boxes, staggering a little under the weight. By the time he finished loading, the Miata's passenger's side and the small space in back of the seats were piled so high that he probably couldn't see out.

Gallegos wasn't just going somewhere, he was moving out. According to Garcia, he went back into the apartment one last time and came out empty handed about five minutes later; probably one last check to make sure that he didn't forget anything. He climbed into the Miata and cranked the ignition. He backed out of the parking area and went down the alley, turning right at the street. He was headed out of town as fast as he could go. Garcia followed when Gallegos turned on the road leading to *Todos Santos* and then on to *La Paz* up the coast. He was still following when he called me.

Adnan Gallegos was getting the hell out of Dodge. Good. I hoped that he'd do just that after our little talk. I tried to put the idea in his empty head by warning not to run, "run" being the operative word. He'd told me everything he knew and now I wanted hm out of the way.

"Okay, stay with him at least to *Todos Santos* and then come on back," I said. "I'll call you later."

I was pleased to be right about how Gallegos would react. It felt most satisfying when I broke into his apartment again. The closet was empty, his computer was gone, and his desk was cleaned out. He left with everything but the furniture and the trash. His landlord would not be happy. Good tenants are hard to find. Of course, I didn't know if Gallegos was a good tenant. He seemed like someone who'd be late with the rent a lot.

Satisfied that Gallegos wouldn't be coming back, I shut the door to the apartment, but left it unlocked. I'd be coming back myself, but this time in the dark. I didn't want to fumble around with the lock. Why make things harder than they had to be?

I intended to take that eleven o'clock call myself.

CHAPTER 24

I WANTED TO BE SURE, so I got to Gallegos's' apartment an hour early after parking a couple of blocks away. I was wearing my burglary best: jeans, a pair of black Nike running shoes, and a black pullover shirt. My gun was tucked in my waistband and I had a pen flashlight and a handkerchief in my pocket.

The night was pitch black. I couldn't even see the rest of me. Gallegos' landlord wasn't exactly generous with exterior lighting. Of course, with tenants skipping out right and left why would he bother? Tenants were such ungrateful bastards. I waited for a moment outside the door. There was no light and no noise from inside. Gallegos' car wasn't in the parking area either.

Just in case, I took out my gun, stepped to one side of the door, turned the knob with my other hand and gave it a gentle push so that it gaped open. I waited for one full minute before stepping inside. Even then I went in at a crouch so that if someone was waiting inside with an anti-tank gun they'd probably fire high and only part my hair.

My caution was unnecessary. The place was as empty as Gallegos's head.

Locking the door behind me, I turned on the flashlight. The curtains were closed and nobody could see in. After checking out the apartment room by room, which took about five seconds, I returned to the bedroom. I sat down on the desk chair, turned off the flashlight so my eyes could get used to the dark, and waited.

It's not easy waiting by yourself in a dark room in an empty apartment, especially when you've committed an illegal act by just being there. I felt like I'd been in Gallegos' place so often lately that I knew it as well as my own. There was a definite shortage of things to do. I caught myself looking at my watch every two minutes. I had to go to the bathroom, too, but that was just nerves. At least that's what I told myself. I decided against seeking relief. In case Gallegos, or somebody else, came in unexpectedly I didn't want to be caught with my pants down. Literally. The obituary would be really embarrassing.

As the minutes crawled by, it became clear that my need to go was more than just nerves. I wondered if Hercule Poirot ever suffered from a full bladder on the job. Probably not. I was pretty sure Miss Marple didn't. Nick and Nora Charles were much too cool to pee. Sherlock Holmes? No chance. Funny, but I couldn't remember Miss Marple's first name. Why did I want to? Who the hell cared?

For all his lack of manly brawn, Gallegos had a surprisingly deep voice. I was pretty sure I could do a fair impersonation of it, at least for a short time over the telephone. It wouldn't fool his mother, but I wasn't expecting his mother to call. If I put a handkerchief over the telephone and pretended to have a cold it might be good enough for what I needed. If it didn't work, I was no worse off than I was before.

More minutes passed. Slowly. Does anybody do impersonations anymore? It occurred to me that I hadn't seen one in years. Of course, who was there to impersonate these days? All the people impersonators used to impersonate were dead. Did anyone replace them? Probably not or there would be more impersonators around. Being a detective, I painstakingly sorted through the evidence and concluded that doing impersonations probably wasn't a growth industry. Fascinating.

As I sat in the dark by myself in a cheap apartment that wasn't mine, waiting for someone I didn't know to call so I could fool them into thinking I was someone else, I decided that Gallegos was the kind of guy who'd answer the telephone with the Spanish equivalent of "yeah" because it sounded tough. After that I'd wing it. I'd already come up with a story about what I'd done all day following myself around. A lot depended on what whoever called had to say. Mostly I wanted to find out who it was and get a sense of what they were after. That might be asking too much, but why not? I'd need a little luck, but whoever it was wouldn't know that they were talking to me, so maybe I could bluff my way into some information? If I failed miserably, like Bob Dylan said, I'd just sorta wasted my precious time. My brain was going around in circles.

I looked at my watch again. It was ten forty five. I wondered if the call would be on time. It was good to be punctual. Good habits are their own reward. Who knows, maybe they'd be early? Maybe I wouldn't have to wait as long as I thought? But what if they were late and I had to wait even longer? Could my bladder hold out? I wasn't sure. I tried not to think about it, which meant that I thought about very little else.

I looked at my watch. It was ten fifty. I was getting better at waiting, no doubt about it. This time I'd waited five whole minutes before looking at my watch. That's what I call progress. Discipline, Cruickshank, discipline.

That's all it takes. You can do it. Attaboy. Buckle down. Apply yourself.

By the time the telephone rang I was nearly incontinent. I expected it, but the sudden jangling sound in the dark made me jump and I forgot all about having to pee.

I lifted the receiver, put my handkerchief over it, and said, "*Sí,*" which wasn't what I originally had in mind but I tried to say it in challenging fashion.

"Gallegos?"

"*Sí,*" I said.

When you've got a good thing going, stay with it.

"You sound funny."

I cleared my throat. "*Tengo un resfriado.*"

Having a cold can explain a lot, I hoped.

"Speak English, dammit!"

"Gotta cold." I coughed for dramatic effect.

"How'd it go today?"

In as few words as possible and in the same awkward phrasing Gallegos used, I did my best imitation. Among other things, I explained that I'd followed myself to the police station, where I stayed all morning. I tried to make it sound boring as hell, which it certainly would have been if it actually happened.

"Yes," the voice said quietly, "that makes sense."

I had the impression that the person on the other end of the line was thinking out loud.

When I finished my brief story about the rest of the day, he said, "Okay."

I coughed into the receiver like tuberculosis was gaining fast.

"What now?"

"What I paid you to do, keep watching," he said. "I'll call tomorrow at the same time."

The line went dead.

The voice sounded familiar from the first syllable, but

I couldn't believe it. When he said, "That makes sense" I knew who it was. "That makes sense" meant that my going to the police station explained something, and that something was why I begged off of my meeting with LaForge, which meant that he knew about our meeting, probably because LaForge told him.

I left the apartment and drove home, stopping to use the bathroom at a McDonald's on the way. Yes, Cabo has a McDonald's. And a lot of other imported American crap. I usually do my best to ignore it, but not this time. There are some things you can count on in this world, and free use of a McDonald's bathroom is one of them.

When I got home, I took a shower. Tired as I was, I knew that it would be a while before I could sleep.

The voice on the other end of the line belonged to Mort Bergman.

CHAPTER 25

I MIXED myself a rum and coke, and sat outside on the patio with the Saltillo tile, listening to the surf pound.

It was warm but still comfortable, with a light breeze coming in off the Gulf of California. The night was clear and the sky was awash in stars, all mixed in swirls and clusters. The moon gave off enough light so that it reflected off the ocean in a shining path to nowhere at all.

"This is strange, kid," I said. "The whole thing is weird. I mean, Mort Bergman?"

"I know," Dina said. "I wish I could be there to help."

"You are. Just hearing your voice helps."

"What are you going to do?"

"I don't know."

"What about the disgruntled wife?"

"Mrs. Bergman?"

"Yes."

"I don't know if she's all that disgruntled. Maybe she was happy to get rid of him."

"But you don't know that she's not either. It might be good to know why they broke up."

"Yeah, you're right," I agreed. "I'll arrange to go north first thing in the morning."

There was a long silence between us. We never minded silence. Sometimes it made us feel closer.

"You know, I can't stay much longer," she said.

"Tonight?"

"No. I mean forever. We've got to let go."

"I don't want to let go. I don't care what the shrink says."

"You have to, Ethan. You can't go on for the rest of your life like this. You've mourned me long enough."

"I'll always mourn you, kid. But you'll always be here, too. I don't see how it can be both ways at the same time, but it is."

"I understand. But I can't let the man I love be miserable for the rest of his life. You can't have me with you forever. I just can't come."

"It's hard. I don't know if I can do it."

"I know it is, but it has to be. I don't know if this is the last time but I do know it's coming soon."

"I love you."

" And I love you. Always have and always will."

I woke up the next morning on the chaise lounge with the sun on my face. The empty glass was on the tiles beside me. I didn't remember falling asleep, or even being sleepy.

CHAPTER 26

THE NEXT MORNING I called Linda Giordano to find out if the Bergman's were living apart. I wanted to talk to Jane Bergman and it would be easier to get to her of they weren't living together.

"Apart as can be," she said. "Mort's got a place here in Cabo, the same corporate condos where I stay when I'm here. Jane's still at the house. California divorce law being what it is I imagine she'll keep it, too."

I called Jane Bergman and told her that I'd been employed to investigate some unusual happenings regarding her husband's place of business and wanted to get her take on a few things. I kept it purposefully vague so she could interpret it any way she wanted. I'd met Jane, but that's all. I needed to get a better sense of her before I said too much. I had to do it in person, too. People often say more with body language than they do with words. And that meant another flight north. Ugh.

"Unusual happenings?" She laughed, but it was not a happy laugh. I'd heard that combination of bitterness, hurt, and anger more than I wanted to back when I handled divorce cases. "Okay, sure, why not? Let's talk."

I'd already checked the flight schedule. If I left now I

could catch a flight, get there, rent a car, drive to her place, talk, and catch a return flight so I could be back here late tonight.

We settled on a time that worked. I was surprised that it was so easy.

"Aren't you an assistant principal, or something?" I asked.

"I took a leave of absence."

I quickly made myself presentable and broke Mexico speed records getting to the airport outside of San Jose del Cabo with a few minutes to spare.

Because I'd booked late I wound up in the dreaded middle seat. It turned out to be okay when the young guy nest to me on the aisle wanted to sit with his sweetie who was in the aisle seat in back of him. I traded with her so they got to hold hands and I got more comfortable.

I wasn't looking forward to my meeting with Jane Bergman and dreaded it every mile on the drive north out of the airport. The Bergmans' house was in a gated community built around a golf course. Both the community and the course were named Quail Hollow. As I remembered it from the only time I was there, the patio in back of the house had a splendid view of the fairway leading to the sixth hole, which was kind of funny because Mort Bergman never golfed in his life. As far as I knew, neither did Jane. Maybe they bought the house for the view? Maybe they liked to watch golfers curse and look for their lost balls? Maybe they just got a good deal?

I gave my name to the uniformed guard at the gate. Full of rent-a-cop self-importance, he frowned and looked at his clipboard as if it held state secrets. He nodded, made an efficient little check mark, raised the gate, and waved me in. I was proud. It's good not to be among the *hoi polloi*. I drove through the curving and hilly streets of Quail Hollow until I came to the

Bergmans' street, appropriately named Winding Way. The red brick ranch-style house was set well back, with an expanse of lawn sloping down to the street. The trees in front were planted when the house was built and had grown enough to shade most of the front lawn.

I wheeled my rented Chevy into the driveway and parked in front of the house. I rang the bell and heard chimes echo inside, immediately followed by the ferocious yapping of a small dog. That was not a good sign. I don't like the ferocious yapping of a small dog.

The door swung open and there stood Jane Bergman with a small and extremely furry creature of uncertain breed cradled in one arm.

It barked at me. Many times. Then it barked some more.

"Don't mind Mitzi," she said, shouting to make herself heard over the barks. "She'll stop in a minute. She just needs to get used to you."

Dina always claimed that Jane Bergman was the kind of woman who could be attractive if she'd only make the effort. Dina wasn't sure if she didn't know how or didn't care, but she was convinced that Jane had vast reservoirs of unrealized potential.

I agreed with the unrealized part. Mostly I thought that no matter how great the effort and expert the application, the result would not have been worth it. Jane Bergman looked like someone who never got word that the sixties were over. Her hair was a long mousy brown, gathered behind her neck by a silver ring. She wore round glasses with silver frames. Her denim skirt revealed calves that had a kind of stringy musculature. The writer Tom Wolfe once described the look as one of "sincere calves." She used to be a serious runner and looked like she was still hard at some kind of rigorous exercise, with a runner's hollow cheeks and skinny arms.

The long sleeves of her white peasant blouse were rolled up past her elbows. She had a silver bracelet on one wrist and a silver watch on the other. With my keen power of observation honed over many years, I concluded that she must like silver.

Still cradling the yapping Mitzi in one arm, with her other arm she reached up and hugged me around the neck. Her hair smelled vaguely of strawberries.

"Ethan, it's been so long," she said. "I can't even remember the last time."

I was hearing a lot of that lately.

"Yeah, it's been a while," I said. "It's good to see you again, Jane."

I followed her into the living room. It was decorated in a pale yellow that had the weird effect of blending everything together. It was the kind of room that would soil easily, but Mitzi wasn't the kind of dog that would dare soil anything. Noise pollution was Mitzi's specialty. She did it well, too.

"Please, sit down," Jane said. "Anywhere you'd like."

I sat on a yellow floral-patterned couch. It was so new or so rarely used that I didn't sink into the cushion at all.

"Can I get you anything?" she asked. "Something to drink?"

"No, thanks," I said, taking a pass on my coffee as an icebreaker ploy.

"Mind if I do?"

"Not at all."

She bent over, gently put Mitzi on the floor and left the room. I heard the refrigerator open and the tinkling of ice in a glass. Mitzi sniffed around my shoes and jumped up on the other end of the couch. She yapped at me two more times before settling in with her tail against the arm of the couch, eying me warily while she waited for a good reason to pounce and rip my throat out.

Jane returned with a tumbler of scotch on the rocks, an interesting way to celebrate the fact that it was early afternoon, and sat in a wing chair decorated in a yellow floral pattern that matched the couch. She crossed her legs, took a belt from her drink, draining about a third of it, and placed it on a plastic coaster on the table next to her chair. At least the amber color of the scotch didn't clash with the rest of the room.

"So what can I do for you?" she asked.

On the drive north from LAX I thought of a dozen ways to get started, but none of them seemed right. When in doubt, tell the truth, at least part of it. I explained that somebody was threatening Jeff LaForge and although the threats weren't necessarily linked to the murder of Jimmy Hopper that was certainly a possibility. I told her that someone had been following me, too. When I accosted them, they cracked under my expert interrogation and revealed that someone who works for Jeff might be involved.

"Who?" she asked.

"I don't know," I replied. "That's part of what I'm trying to find out."

"What do you want from me?"

It was a good question. I wasn't sure myself.

"Look, Jane, I don't want to make what must be a difficult time even worse, but I need to know about Mort," I said. "I'm not saying he's involved in any of this. I'm asking around about everybody. I don't know when you separated or what caused it, but I was wondering if you'd noticed anything out of the ordinary, any peculiar or unusual behavior on his part, if he said anything that struck you as strange, or if he mentioned anything like that at work. I probably even want to know what caused your breakup, but I'm too much of a gentleman to ask, which is sort of a backward way of asking exactly that."

I accompanied that last comment with what I hoped was a winning yet rueful smile. I threw in a dash of disarming, too. It probably looked like a grimace, but at least I was trying.

"Out of the ordinary?" She laughed the same bitter laugh as before, only this time there was touch of hysteria, too. Jane Bergman was not in a good way. I had the impression that she was just barely hanging on.

She finished her drink in another large gulp. "When you called earlier you said 'unusual occurrences.' Now it's 'out of the ordinary.' I guess either one works, doesn't it?"

"How do you mean?" I asked.

"Would you call it 'out of the ordinary' or an 'unusual occurrence' if your husband of more than twenty five years was obsessed with another woman?" she asked.

There was no possible answer to that question. I had the good sense not to try to offer one.

Jane got up, walked into the kitchen, and returned with another scotch. She sat down, took another drink, carefully placed the glass on the plastic coaster, just like before, and smoothed out her denim skirt.

"She seduced him, of course. I mean, you know Mort. He's no ladies man. Until her, I was the only woman he ever had. The first time was years ago. I didn't know it until he confessed. He said he was heartbroken by what he'd done. I believed him. He was so far out of his league that he didn't even understand how it happened. The poor fool never had a chance against her. When he promised me it would never happen again, I believed that, too. I think he even believed it."

I didn't say anything. Even Mitzi shut up. Jane took another drink. The ice rattled in the glass. It was almost empty already. While she drank, I asked myself: Who in the hell would bother to seduce Mort Bergman?

"I worried for a while, for a long time, really. But when she got married I stopped worrying. These things happen to people. I know that. Not even I'm immune. There are men in this world who find me attractive, if I do say so myself. Mort's not the only one. You'd be surprised if I named names. Mort doesn't know what he's lost."

I let that pass, too. I was starting to feel like I wasn't in the room at all.

"Then it happened again. I think she did it for sport, just because she could. She enjoyed playing with him. He was like a fish on a line. Mort admitted that he was obsessed with her, and had been ever since the first time. He never stopped thinking about her. But this time he didn't confess, I caught them. I had a conference that day. Several of us from the school district met with some people from the state superintendent's office at the Hyatt. Mort didn't know about the meeting, or maybe he forgot that I told him. Anyway, I was in the lobby when they came down the stairs after a nice little nooner. The slut didn't even care. She just smiled and kept walking like nothing had happened. Mort was too stunned to say anything. He practically ran away. I got a lawyer the next day and threw him out of the house. I haven't told anyone except the lawyer but I guess these things get around pretty fast."

She was crying and probably didn't even know it. Huge tears rolled down her face and dripped on her blouse, leaving big wet marks. There were no sobs or sniffles. She didn't reach for anything to wipe the tears away. The pain was all there was. That and the scotch. She lived everyday with knives tearing at her heart and didn't know how to make it stop.

"She used my husband and when she was finished she threw him away like he was trash. She ruined our marriage and didn't give a damn. Mort said she laughed when he told her we were through. She's probably moved on to the next victim by now."

I tried to think of something to say and came up empty. "I'm sorry" seemed so trite that I didn't want to insult her by saying it.

For the first time in a while, she looked me in the eye, her own eyes glistened with tears and her wet face shined in the light.

"Don't you want to know who it was?"

"Yeah, I do," I said.

"It was that man-eating bitch Abby LaForge."

She was too distraught to notice what must have been an amazing look on my face, probably some goofy combination of stupefaction and paralysis. In a strange way, I think I expected it. The more she'd talked about this extraordinary *femme fatale* the more it sounded like Abby, the evil Abby and not the decent human being Abby that lived in the same person. But I still couldn't believe it when she said the name. Abby LaForge and Mort Bergman? It was too ridiculous to be true, except that it was. Hell, why not Mort Bergman and Jennifer Lopez? Or Mort Bergman and Margaret Thatcher?

And exactly where did this get me, other than a first row ticket to a real life soap opera? As I sat in Jane Bergman's yellow living room and watched her drink and cry, with the pain in her heart practically bursting out of her chest, if there was some link between Mort and Abby doing the horizontal hula and Mort having me followed I sure as hell didn't see it.

I could have asked more questions but by now Jane was in no condition to provide coherent answers. I stayed another half hour while she got drunk, thanks to two more scotches. By the time I got up to leave she'd begun to blubber. Her Ss were sloshing together and she had a hard time getting out of the chair to see me to the door.

"You dunno how terr'ble ish been," she said, leaning against the door jam for support. Mitzi was at her feet. When Jane bent down and scooped her up I was afraid that she might fall over.

"No," I said. "I probably don't. It isn't fair that you had to tell me about it either."

She hugged me again when I said goodbye, leaving me with a wet shoulder. When I backed out of the driveway she was still leaning against the door jam holding Mitzi the Wonder Dog in her arms.

CHAPTER 27

ABBY AND MORT BERGMAN!

As tired as I was after a day of travel, my brain wouldn't stop working, not on the drive to LAX, not on the flight, and not at home. It just didn't compute.

And even if it did, what was I supposed to do with it? Everything in this case seemed to add up to less than the sum of its parts.

I couldn't very well go to Jeff LaForge and say, "Thanks to my peerless investigation, I know that your wife screwed your long-time number two man at least twice, ruined his marriage, and turned his wife into a lush. Not only that, he had me followed by an idiot. By the way, where's my check?"

I THOUGHT it through one more time in case I'd missed something: Unless you're Jane Bergman, Mort paying Gallegos to follow me is more significant than what happened between Mort and Abby. Jeff hired me to find out who was threatening him, not to keep track of his wife's sex life. So far I'd managed to find out about every-thing but what he hired me to find out.

I was frustrated, angry, disappointed and a lot of other things. Everything seemed to be piling up in all the wrong places and I didn't like any of it. Being a private detective was a lot easier when the bad stuff doesn't involve people I know.

CHAPTER 28

I CALLED GARCIA. We agreed to meet on his lunch break at a hole in the wall restaurant on the highway connecting Cabo San Lucas with San José del Cabo. I'd probably driven past a hundred times without really seeing it. According to Garcia, it was a popular working man's hangout, meaning that it was cheap and fast. We agreed to meet at eleven forty five to beat the crowd.

I wore jeans, black loafers, a white pullover shirt, and my ankle rig. A skinny waitress with magenta hair, a pierced nose, and a tattooed neck waved me to a table and slapped a couple of plastic menus down.

Garcia showed up about ten minutes later, dressed in his dark brown gardener's outfit. I always wondered why landscaping people dressed like that since they worked in the hot sun all day. It had been interesting to watch Garcia change and grow from the night we met at the restaurant. The diffident young man who wasn't sure of himself and desperately hoped to land a gig with me had regained his old cop attitude. Most cops have a certain way about them. They're usually confident, but even if they're not, they act like it. They're used to confrontation and like to give the impression that they're a step ahead of everybody else. The way Garcia carried himself said that no matter what you were thinking, he already knew about it. A cop needs that ability to intimidate, to get the psychological upper hand and keep it is an important part of self-defense. Sometimes it's the most effective part.

I made a mental note to tell Garcia to tone it down a little. An aggressive, in your face gardener tends to stand out.

The waitress reappeared. I ordered iced tea. Garcia ordered coffee and a soft drink. She left to get our drinks while I checked out the plastic menu. When she returned, I ordered a couple of shrimp tacos. Garcia ordered a hamburger with fries.

I watched her walk away. Most waitresses have the same walk, especially in cheap restaurants, no matter where they are. It's a combination of speed and resignation.

About two minutes later, our food appeared. Nobody said anything, but it was clear that the management did not want us lingering over our meal. There would be no savoring a fine post-meal port. When you run a restaurant that's basically a collection of tables and umbrellas to provide minimum shade, rapid customer turnover is everything.

"Okay, here's what's happened since we last talked and what I think I know so far …."

I told him about what happened at the party after we talked. I told him about Gallegos and about breaking into his apartment multiple times. I told him about finding my name on a list in his computer and about the envelope in his trash. I told him about the discussion in his Miata and about going back to his apartment and hearing Mort Bergman's voice on the telephone. I told him about my conversation with Linda Giordano, what I knew about the relationship between Abby and Jeff LaForge, and how they apparently were not the happy couple they seemed to be in public, a conclusion that Garcia's own observations seemed to enforce. I told him everything I knew about Mort Bergman, the state of the Bergman's marriage, and that the Bergmans were no longer a couple at all. And I told him why.

Some of what I told him Garcia already knew, but a lot of it he didn't. He took a deep breath. His cheeks inflated while he blew the air out. He threw one arm over the back of his chair. Looking out somewhere into the middle distance, he thought about everything I said. He drank more coffee, put the cup down, leaned forward, and put his forearms on the table.

"Speaking as a highly trained former officer of the Mexico City *policia*, there's not much in all of this to move on officially, or even unofficially," he said.

I noticed that even Garcia's speech was less boyish and more professional than when we first met. His English was better, too, as if he felt that it made him seem more professional when dealing with me, the gringo. All he needed was a chance. I was glad I gave it to him.

"Unless it becomes stalking, having someone followed isn't necessarily illegal. Since all you had to do was blow on Gallegos to scare him away, the stalking thing wouldn't work even if you wanted it to. It wouldn't matter anyway. He doesn't know anything more than what he told you. Gallegos probably could make better case against you than you could against him."

Garcia took another bite of his hamburger and followed it with a final gulp of coffee.

"But you are right," he said. "It's all connected somehow."

"You haven't seen or heard anything new on your end have you?" I asked.

"No." He shook his head. "I haven't seen or heard the woman in at least a day."

A final bite of his hamburger. I'd finished my tacos long ago.

"This Bergman … in this country, we'd have taken him in by now, even if we didn't have much."

"In this country, you do lots of interesting things," I said. "You're referring to the possibility that he probably thinks that he's done a lot more for business than Jeff LaForge ever did and so why the hell isn't he rich, too. And maybe he let that fester inside for years. And now he's obsessed by LaForge's wife, a woman with whom he's had a previous sexual relationship, even though it sounds like she treats him like pond scum and that probably pisses him off, too? Yes, I'd say he looks pretty good. But I don't think that I have enough to tell Jeff."

"Say we're right," Garcia said. "Why now?"

"The girl," I said. "Abby. The second time sent him over the edge."

"Here's another one," Garcia said. "What if this Mrs. Bergman isn't telling the truth?"

"Jane? You mean about her husband and LaForge's wife?" I asked.

He nodded.

"Why would she make it up?" I asked. "From what she told me it's so unlikely that's it's gotta be true, unless she's into some kind of fantasy self abuse and likes being a victim."

"Sometimes lushes invent things and don't even know they're inventing them," he said. "Maybe she needs to think that somebody else ruined her marriage, that it wasn't about her. How bad is the drinking?"

"I'd say it's recent, the bad part anyway," I said. "It probably comes from the hurt. I don't think it's permanent. As the hurt passes, assuming it does, so will the drinking."

"If she's telling the truth, what does this have to do with the man who was murdered?" he asked.

"You know, I can see Bergman making the threats, sort of," I said. "There's a kind of weird logic to it, even if I still don't understand what he's supposed to get out of it. But you're right. Hopper doesn't fit. Neither do those bozos in the parking lot. And why have me followed?"

"Maybe he wanted to find out what you know," Garcia said. "But that doesn't explain the three *hombres* at the restaurant. Maybe he wanted you to stop looking? A broken leg would do it. Bergman may be it. But you knew that already. I think that you don't want it to be Bergman because you feel sorry for him."

"You're pretty smart for a gardener," I said.

"I hope to work my way up in the world."

I paid the check, including a big tip for the crackerjack service and exciting body art, and we left.

Next time we'd meet somewhere else. Sometimes cheap is still too expensive.

And I was glad to be working with Ramon Garcia. I liked the kid.

CHAPTER 29

SINCE EVERYTHING, or a lot of it, pointed to Mort Bergman, and nothing pointed to anybody else, I decided to follow Bergman. Garcia was right. Part of me wanted to catch him at something he shouldn't be doing. The rest of me didn't want to.

I got the standard equipment ready the night before: binoculars, a camera with short, medium and long lenses, spare batteries for the camera, a notebook, a couple of pens, a flashlight with extra batteries, and two different kinds of sunglasses, one pair of Ray-Ban aviators and a pair of wrap-around Oakleys. I put a jacket in the back seat in case I wound up someplace where I needed one. I already had two hats in the car. One was the usual baseball cap. The other was a straw riverboat gambler's hat. With all that, I had lots of different looks.

In the morning I made a couple of sandwiches from some left over meat loaf, wrapped each one in its own little baggie and put them in a small cooler, along with a thermos full of ice chips.

By six, I was parked at a corner near Bergman's place, one of the corporate condos that lined one side of the block, the same complex where Linda Giordano lived when she was in Cabo, although I didn't know which condo was hers. The car Bergman drove in Cabo, a white Ford Fusion, was parked on the street.

Tailing someone you know is more difficult than tailing a stranger, which is why I brought all the hats and sunglasses. I'd have to stay at a greater distance than I normally would, but if I didn't get sloppy or have some bad luck I'd be all right. There was no reason for Bergman to think I was tailing him, so he wouldn't be looking. I decided not to rent a different car, although I kept the top up on the Mustang so that at a distance it would look like a hard top...

Ninety minutes later, looking spiffy in a gray suit and white shirt with no tie and carrying a black briefcase, Bergman walked out of the condo to his Ford.

I followed as he drove to his office and parked next to LaForge's empty spot along the side of the building where the brass parked. LaForge's place had his name on it. Bergman's didn't. I bet it rankled Bergman every time he went to work. I used to think he was unflappable. I knew better now.

I drove slowly past the entrance as Bergman entered the building. Watching through the glass doors, I saw him pass the redoubtable guard and head up the escalator. Unless Bergman had changed his habits, he was going up to the third-floor cafeteria to get a cup of coffee before heading to his office.

It was early and I had plenty of choices for parking. I picked a spot a block and a half from the entrance. It was far enough away that I wouldn't be spotted but still close enough so I could watch the entrance *and* the only exit from the parking lot. I'd change my position a couple of times during the day. The change would make me harder to spot and help alleviate boredom at least for a few minutes.

It was going to be another hot day but I couldn't run the air conditioner because I didn't want to run down the battery. On the other hand, I could always hope that Bergman wouldn't hang around the office all day.

He did. The only time he left was to attend a lunch meeting at one of the hotels along the marina. Bergman was a long-time member of Rotary and I followed him until he went inside to eat a bad lunch and share the secret handshake, or whatever it is Rotarians do when they're not singing their jolly Rotarian songs and doing good Rotarian deeds.

After lunch, I followed him back to the office. After finding another spot that gave me the view I wanted, I spent the rest of the day doing nothing.

Early that evening, Bergman walked out of the building, his suit jacket over his shoulder... He got in his Ford and drove home. It was ten minutes after seven, just another eleven hours-plus day at the office for Mort Bergman. LaForge usually came to work later and left earlier. The chances were good that Bergman noticed it, too.

Bergman's workday might be finished, but I wasn't that lucky. I followed him home and sat in the car as it got dark and watched the lights turn on in his condo, first on the ground floor, then upstairs.

I'd eaten my sandwiches, chewed all my ice, and drank the water when the ice melted. The more I resolved not to think about how hungry and thirsty I was the hungrier and thirstier I was. My butt hurt, my head hurt, and there was no comfortable position left for me to try. I was so sick of my own car I was ready to sell it.

At ten thirty the light on the ground floor went out. The light on the second floor followed twenty minutes later. I drove down the alley in back of the condo to make sure all the lights were off. They were. I parked out front again and waited another forty five minutes to be sure that Bergman had wrapped up the day.

When I was confident that I'd waited along enough, I got out and walked to his car. I could hear the joints in my stiff knees crackle as I walked. Using an ice pick, I jabbed a small hole in his left rear tail light, careful not to break the bulb inside. If I had to follow him at night, that little hole would make it a lot easier too keep some distance away.

Pleased with my vandalism, I drove home. I hadn't worn either of my hats or the Oakley sunglasses. I was saving those thrills for tomorrow, something to brighten up the day.

I made myself a roast beef sandwich and drank two beers. I grabbed a towel, walked out to the patio stark naked, and dove in the pool. Doing nothing wore me out. I felt like I'd gone two out of three falls with a Tyrannosaurus Rex. I took another beer with me to the pool, although, technically speaking, none of them were beers. Never underestimate the medicinal properties of Boddington's Ale. It's been known to work miracles.

After thirty minutes of swimming and floating, I climbed out and toweled myself off. I went up the stairs to the bedroom and slid into bed.

As Scarlet O'Hara said, tomorrow is another day. I wasn't looking forward to it either, not if it was anything like this one.

CHAPTER 30

AFTER TWO MORE DAYS I reached the conclusion that Mort Bergman was the most boring man in the world.

He worked long hours. He had lunch with an underling from work. Bergman had a salad. The underling had some kind of fish. Even with binoculars, I was too far away to see what kind. He swam laps at the pool at his condo. He went to the *mercado* and bought groceries. He bought gas. I didn't see why because he never went anywhere.

That was it. By the end of the third day I was so bored I felt like I must be losing my mind. My attitude wasn't very professional. Sometimes a tail can last for weeks. But it was the only attitude I had.

Breaking and entering had worked so well with Gallegos that I decided to try it again. After Bergman left for work on the fourth day I called Linda Giordano's cell phone from my car.

"Hey, Toots, the name's Bond, James Bond," I said.

"Toots?" she said. "Toots? I am no Toots."

"That's okay," I said. "I'm not James Bond either."

"How disappointing," she said. "What do you want?"

"The usual," I said. "You know, a favor."

"I kind of guessed that since a favor is all you ever want," she said. "What is it this time?"

"You're still here in Cabo, right?"

"Right."

"If Mort leaves the building, the very second he leaves the building, would you call me?" I said. "You won't even have to talk to me. I just want you to call if he leaves."

"That sounds like something I can handle," she said.

"Thanks, Toots."

"Sure thing, double o seven. Watch your ass."

If Linda called while I was in mid burgle I'd see her number on my phone and have time to get out of Bergman's condo. I could always re-burgle later.

I didn't know what I was looking for but I was sick of sitting on my butt. Doing something and not finding anything is a lot better than doing nothing and not finding anything. I think.

I got my kit out of the trunk and walked down the unpaved alley in back of Bergman's condo. Another line of identical condos backed up to the alley and fronted on the next street. A six-foot stucco wall ran along the backs of both lines of condos, with one wooden gate for each unit. When I got to Bergman's place I stood on my toes and looked over the wall. Each unit had its own little backyard, complete with a lovely cement patio slightly smaller than a postage stamp. Bergman's green area had no green at all unless you counted the weeds shooting up out of the dirt. The tiny patio was bare except for a single white plastic chair, the kind you can buy at any drug store for about eight bucks. There was something sad about it. It was more than neglect. It was indifference.

If Bergman had a lock on his back gate I'd either have to climb over the wall or break in through the front door. Climbing over the wall wasn't a problem but I didn't want to do it I didn't have to. If somebody saw me they might call the cops. I didn't want to break in through the front door either. It was a little too public in the daylight.

Fortunately Bergman's sense of security was not finely tuned. The gate was unlocked. The bad news was that it sagged on its hinges so when I opened the gate it made a loud scraping sound on the cement walk. It was too late to do anything about it now. I walked in like I was supposed to be there, bounded up the three steps and began working on the lock. It was a little tougher than the lock at Gallegos's apartment, but not much. Although it seemed like longer because I felt more vulnerable than I did at Gallegos's place, it took less than a minute to get in.

With Bergman gone, I was confident there was no one inside. In three days, I hadn't seen anyone else come or go.

The back door put me in the kitchen. As usual, I did a fast walk through the place to get a sense of the layout. The dining room was to the right of the kitchen, with the living room in front of that. There was a coat closet and a small half-bath off the living room.

I went upstairs and glanced in each room without taking in the details. There were two bedrooms and two bathrooms upstairs, with one of the bathrooms adjoining the master bedroom. While it was a lot nicer than Gallegos' dump, the condo still had all the charm of a motel. The furniture all matched and looked fairly new. The corporation probably rented it. Instant lifestyle.

I went back downstairs and started working my way up. Mort Bergman read Time magazine, the Los Angeles Times, and the Wall Street Journal, all of them brought home from the office, according to the address label. A half-dozen books were scattered around the living room, four on the coffee table and two more on an end table.

With the exception of a Tom Clancy novel, all of them were business-related non-fiction. The exception was one of Clancy's early novels, the one about the submarine. There was no meat in the refrigerator, but there were a lot of fruit and vegetables. There was no beer, but there was a bottle of medium-priced scotch on the tile counter next to the refrigerator. The trash was in a plastic wastebasket under the kitchen sink, or it would have been if Bergman had any trash. He probably took it out last night or early this morning before he went to work. I'd noticed a big green dumpster in the alley in back of the condos.

Upstairs, the bed was so neatly made you could bounce a quarter on it. It was a theme that carried over into the rest of the room. Most people are neat about the part visitors can see and a little sloppy about the rest, often more than a little. Bergman seemed to be just the opposite. His closet was so neat there was a kind of obsessive geometric precision to it. Counting the one he wore this morning, Bergman kept nine suits in Cabo, ranging from gray all the way to black. The hangers were perfectly aligned and everything hung perfectly on the hangers. The pants were creased just so and the shirts were buttoned all the way to the top. It was the same with his shoes. Not one was out of line. They stood there like good little soldiers waiting for duty. His shaving cream, razor and deodorant were neatly arranged on the glass counter above the sink in the bathroom. His boxer shorts were perfectly stacked in the dresser drawer. So were his socks. The shorts appeared to have been ironed or taken to a dry cleaners, which was taking neatness entirely too far. The wastebasket in the bathroom was empty, just like the one downstairs.

It seemed to me that Mort Bergman was more than a touch anal, but that only confirmed what I already suspected. Besides, judging by the life he seemed to live, what the hell else did he have to do? Keeping his shoes in line probably was the high point of his day.

He used the second bedroom as an office. There was a small metal desk against one wall, with a window on the other wall to the right of the desk that overlooked the alley and the condos on the other side. There was a large cork bulletin board sitting on the desk and leaning against the wall. It was covered with photographs of Abby LaForge. I heard myself gasp. There were so many it was hard to focus on just one. A few looked like posed photographs, but in most it was clear that she didn't know her picture was being taken. There were shots of Abby looking at a store window, Abby walking, Abby in her car, Abby jogging, and several of Abby in her home, a few with Abby in various stages of undress, and a couple where she had no clothes at all. In one, Abby and Jeff were having full-bore sex, which they appeared to be enjoying immensely. They were on the sofa in the sun room. Jeff was lying on his back and Abby was astride him, with her knees on either side of his hips. Her back was arched and her head was tilted back. His hands were on her breasts and his mouth was open. He was probably bellowing like a moose.

The house photos appeared to have been taken from outside. In a couple, I could see the outline of a window frame. With others, I was familiar enough with the house to know that he either had to be standing in the room or outside shooting through the window. I doubted that even the LaForges were kinky enough to invite Mort Bergman into their home to take pictures of their sex life.

Despite the nudity and the sex, the photo collection was strangely non-sexual. It had all the allure of an archi-tect's rendering of a cafeteria. The whole thing made me feel like a peeping Tom and I wasn't even the one doing the original peeping. I was sweating, but I felt clammy, too. I could feel my heart pounding and there was a loud ringing in my ears.

Jane told me, but I didn't really believe it. Mort Bergman was a man obsessed, and he was obsessed with Abby LaForge. I shouldn't have been surprised, but I was.

I went through the desk and metal filing cabinet next to the desk drawer-by-drawer and item-by-item, but my eyes kept going back to the bulletin board. I saw one photo where I was sure Bergman was in the room when he took it. Abby was in bed. There was no way to tell if it was in the LaForge house, a hotel room, or somewhere on the island of Cyprus. She was naked, lying on her side with her legs bent and one hand across her knees. Her head was cocked in her other hand, with her elbow resting on the pillow. The shot was taken from down toward the foot of the bed. Her whole attitude, everything from her body language to the self-satisfied half smile on her face, screamed sex. Whether she just had it, wanted it, or both, I couldn't tell.

There was another element, too. It took me a minute to figure it out. It was the look on her face. It was as if she was taunting the photographer.

I turned on Bergman's computer and checked the files, but didn't see anything interesting. In a way, I was relieved. I'd already seen more than I wanted to.

After one more pass through the condo to make sure I hadn't missed anything, I locked the back door, shut it, passed through the tiny yard and walked out the gate into the alley. This time I lifted the gate as I opened and closed it so it wouldn't make any more noise. I walked up the alley, turned right, walked to Bergman's street, turned left and walked to the Mustang.

I unlocked the door, tossed my bag in the back seat and got in. I'd parked under a tree and it was cool in the car. My heart was pounding and my hands still felt clammy. I took several deep breaths to try to calm down. Finally I leaned forward and put my forehead on the steering wheel. I'd just seen one of the ugliest sights of my life.

CHAPTER 31

FROM MY CAR, I called Garcia and took him off gardening duty. I was sick of watching Bergman even before I broke into his condo. After what I'd just seen I didn't want to have to look at him any more than I had to for a while.

I described Bergman in detail, including the address of his condo, told Garcia where I'd be, and drove over to Bergman's office. Linda Giordano hadn't called, so he still must be hard at work. After a forty-five minute wait, Garcia slowly cruised down the street. He saw me and, without acknowledging each other, I moved out of my parking spot so he could move in.

For no particular reason I decided to drive out to the LaForge house. Linda Giordano said Jeff should be at home, although he had appointments later. I didn't have anything in mind, but I could always say something about checking in. After all, Jeff was my client. It was something I should do anyway.

I wheeled into the driveway and pulled up to the house. LaForge's Lexus was parked in front of the house. I got out of the car, walked up to the door, and rang the bell.

LaForge answered the door. He was wearing tan

cargo pants, deck shoes and a red LaCoste pullover shirt with the tail hanging out.

"Ethan," he said. "What a surprise. Nothing bad, I hope."

"Not lately," I said. "I just thought I'd stop by. I haven't checked in with you in a while."

"Come on in," he said. "I think there's some coffee left. Want some?"

LaForge turned back into the house, with me tagging along behind.

"Jeff, you sure it's not too early?"

LaForge laughed as we walked into the kitchen. "No, it's fine. I was just gonna shower, dress, and go to the office. How'd you know I was home?"

"I called Linda," I said.

There was just enough coffee left in the pot for two cups. "Cream? Sugar?"

I shook my head and accepted a cup and saucer.

"Where's the household help?"

"She's off today and Abby's working out, I think. She goes in real early four or five times a week, regular as hell. She does ... oh, what do you call it? Zumba, some core stuff, and a little weight work."

LaForge led the way into the sun room. He sat on the couch. I took a chair. After the photograph I'd seen at Bergman's condo I wanted no part of the couch anyway.

"I don't even know what Zumba it is exactly," he continued. "But judging by the result, I'd say it works for her. She's got a butt like iron."

I nodded my admiration of his wife's butt. Man talk was such fun.

LaForge took a sip of coffee. He sighed contentedly and sat the cup and saucer on the coffee table. I did the same thing, but without the phony sigh.

"What can I do for you?" he asked. "Anything you need from me?"

I shook my head. "Like I said, I'm just checking in, that's all. I know you haven't reported anything, but I always like to hear and see for myself."

LaForge gave a dismissive little shrug. "There's been nothing to report. I guess that's good news, isn't it?"

He ran his long fingers through his hair. It fell back into place as though he'd never disturbed it.

"To tell you the truth, I'm nervous as hell," he admitted. "I mean, we both are. Any unusual noise makes us jump. Neither one of has been sleeping that well either. We were reading in bed a few nights ago when one of the circuit breakers went out and the room suddenly went dark. I must have jumped three feet off the bed. A couple of times I've had the feeling that somebody's watching, but I look around and nobody's there. It's probably just paranoia. Abby feels the same way. We laugh about it, but it gets to you after a while, you know? We even went out to the shooting range to get in a little target practice, though I don't know what good it's supposed to do. I hadn't fired a gun in years."

"If you're thinking about buying a gun, Mexico has pretty strict laws about that," I said.

Jeff took a sip of coffee. "I've got contacts, the best, really. I got one okay."

"When does Abby get home?"

"You know, I'm not sure." He held the cup and saucer in front of his chest while he drank. "With the new facility here, a deal for another one in Mexico I'm working on, and all the business travel I'm doing, I'm so damn busy I can go for a long time and not even see my wife. I know that after she works out she likes to hang around and have some juice or something with the girls, maybe a little breakfast, too. You know how that goes."

"Not really," I said. "It's been a while since I've had any juice with the girls."

LaForge laughed. The laugh told me that he didn't think I was funny, but one has to observe the social niceties.

As his fake laughter died, he glanced at his watch, the usual eight-pound Rolex.

"I should get moving. I've got a meeting." He rolled his eyes. "I've always got a damn meeting. Most of 'em aren't worth having. Even so, I'd better get ready. I still have to shower and dress."

He rose to his feet.

"I guess I haven't been much help, have I?"

I got up, too.

"Like I said, I was just checking in. Tell Abby I dropped by, would you? If either one of you needs to reach me, you know how. Anytime. Like the Pinkertons, I never sleep. At least that's what I tell clients."

We shook hands. We were both glad it was over. If the conversation was any more forced we'd be in handcuffs.

"Thanks for coming by," he said. "I'll tell Abby you were here. This whole thing's been pretty tough. We're not used to it."

"Nobody is," I said.

I told him that I could find my own way out and he let me. I didn't mention that I'd seen pictures of the two of them getting it on in the room I'd just left. Some things are best left unspoken.

CHAPTER 32

"So you were shocked?" he asked in his usual calm and reasonable voice.

"I sure as hell was," I said. "Who wouldn't be?"

"It takes a lot to shock you," he said. "At least that's what you like to believe."

"What do you mean, 'that's what you like to believe'?"

We were talking on the telephone. Even at long distance, I usually felt at ease almost immediately. But not this time.

"You think of yourself as more cynical than you are," he said. "I know that, I think you know that, and it's likely that anyone who knows you well knows that. You bury feelings you don't like so that you won't have to deal with them and then hide it under a crust of cynicism that doesn't go very deep."

"Okay, let's say you're right." I knew he was right, but I didn't want to admit it. "What does that have to do with what's going on?" I knew the answer to that already. I was just being a cranky pain in the ass.

"You've seen and heard too many things that you

didn't want to see and hear involving people you know pretty well," he explained. "That's never a pleasant experience."

"But I wasn't close to any of them," I protested.

"You said yourself that you thought Mort Bergman was a good man. While it's true that you dislike Abby's husband, your feelings about her are ambivalent. You even admire her in a way. "

"I'm not sure I admire her," I said. "Especially now."

"You admire intelligence and independence and she seems to have both," he said. "The fact that's she an attractive woman only adds to the mix. You may not like what she's done, but that's a different thing, and, despite the photographs, you don't really know the circumstances."

I didn't say anything. The circumstances seemed pretty obvious to me.

"You didn't have an episode when you saw the photographs?" he asked.

"No."

"Any symptoms?'

"No."

"How did you feel?"

"Bad," I said. "I'm sick of these people and how they're acting. I guess I haven't sorted it out yet. What I saw wasn't pleasant for a lot of reasons, but there was something more, too."

"I know. There may be a feeling of betrayal here," he said. "It's something we'll have to explore."

"Yes," I said, "I guess we will."

"Have you given any thought to what we talked about last time?"

"You mean, be sad, but not for too long"?

He nodded.

"Yes," I replied, "I have. I'm not sure what to do about it, but I have given it a lot of thought.. Maybe Dina can help."

"Maybe," he said.

CHAPTER 33

I DROVE TO THE CLUB, changed clothes and worked out. I never really enjoyed working out but I didn't feel social enough for tennis. I wasn't in the mood to talk to anybody. A couple of people I knew nodded hello while I was huffing and puffing on the Nautilus. I ignored them.

For once, the workout felt good. The mindless activity was just what I needed.

A long time ago, I read a magazine story about body-builders. Not the professionals, the guys who have regular jobs and hit the gym after work and on weekends.

One of the saddest things I ever read came from a good-looking young guy whose physique was breathtaking, judging by the photographs, especially when you consider the thousands of hours of work it took to make it that way. It was as if every muscle in his body was perfectly defined. He was so far from normal human development that he had to have his clothes specially made.

He sold medical supplies for a living. He explained that he liked working out because the rest of the time he had to be the kind of man "they" wanted him to be.

Working out and sculpting his body, he could be the kind of man he wanted to be.

For some reason, that stayed with me. I hoped the poor guys' life was better now. Who knows? Maybe he was fifty pounds overweight and happy as hell? Or maybe he put a gun in his mouth and blew his brains out?

After an hour, I was so pumped up I felt like Hercules. I cooled down for about ten minutes, walked into the locker room, threw my shirt and shorts on the floor, and hit the shower. I stood for a long time with my head leaning against the tile wall underneath the faucet, letting the hot water work on my neck and shoulders.

I toweled myself off and dressed in jeans, a light blue pullover shirt and black loafers with no socks. Once I combed my hair I was ready for action.

Almost. I didn't want to alarm the locker room, so I waited until I got out to the car to strap on the ankle holster.

I drove home and started on some busy work. There were a couple of calls from insurance companies that wanted to employ me, and another from an attorney who wanted the same thing.

It occurred to me that I'd received more offers of employment in the last week or ten days than I got in the last six months. Either business was picking up or they had me confused with somebody else.

I returned the calls. One insurance company needed someone right away, which let me out. The other one said it would be at least a month before my services were required, so I said yes. The attorney was a guy I'd worked for once before. He wanted to know if I was interested in investigating somebody his client was about to sue. He wasn't sure how much he'd need me because the case might be settled out of court, but was I available if necessary? I gave him a definite maybe and we agreed to talk later.

I put my feet up, leaned back in the chair, and tried for some bikini sightings. Even with binoculars, I had no luck.

I didn't have anything scheduled and, although I'd never admit this to a client, I didn't know what to do next. The Jimmy Hopper murder kept whirling around in my head. Did it have anything to do with what I was supposed to be working on? If it did, who knew what Jimmy Hopper was doing that day?

Hopper himself, of course. Did he arrange to meet somebody and something went wrong and they killed him? Some kind of drug thing maybe?

I didn't believe that for a second. Stranger things have happened, but I still didn't believe it. But if not drugs, then what? Gambling? I didn't believe that either. Neither gambling nor drugs fit with what I knew and heard about Hopper.

Did Hopper call anybody before he was killed? Cell phone records would show that easy enough. I was sure the police had checked it out and made a mental note to ask Hauser.

Did Bergman or LaForge have anything to do with it? Why would either one of them want one of their own people killed? Why would *anybody* want Hopper killed? The question put me back on square one.

There *was* a common link, though, and that was Abby LaForge. She was married to Jeff, she had an affair, or something, with Mort, and she was pals with Hopper, plus a lot of people thought that she'd had or was having an affair with him. I could even add Jane Bergman to the mix if I wanted to.

Making no progress whatsoever, I decided that I was hungry and went to the kitchen. Standing at the counter, I made myself a sandwich out of leftover lamb, lettuce, pickles, onions, mustard and dark rye bread. I went outside and sat at the table, where I drank a glass of red wine and ate my sandwich. I liked it so much that I made another one. I ate and read outside until it was too dark to see the words. I went inside to see if I could find a movie to watch on the satellite.

As often happened, I'd already seen the good ones and wasn't interested in the bad ones. There wasn't anything on the History Channel, so I settled for watching two movies at once, switching back and forth from a good part in one movie to a good part in another. It used to drive Dina stark raving mad when I did that. Someone once said that women are interested in what's on TV. Men are interested in what *else* is on TV.

By ten I was considering going to bed, except that I felt too lazy to get out of the chair. The next thing I knew the cell phone in my pocket was making noise. It was a moment before I realized that I'd fallen asleep. A glance at my watch told me that it was just past midnight.

"Hello," I said.

"It's Valencia."

His voice jolted me awake. Cops don't call late at night with good news. In fact, nobody calls late at night with good news.

"Yeah," I said.

"Someone shot Abby LaForge."

I went blank for a second. It was as if something clicked off inside my head.

"She's dead," he said.

CHAPTER 34

IT WAS A LOCATION, not an address - a long and lonely stretch of two-lane road about thirty minutes north and east of Cabo San Lucas.

The streets outside of town were empty. Barreling along at eighty miles an hour, it didn't take me long to get there. I pulled off the road and got out of the Mustang. Weeds were knee high and thick on both sides of the road, which was slightly elevated over the land around it. On the right side of the road where I parked in the darkness the weeds ran about fifty yards or more to some scrubby cactus. At least I thought it was scrubby cactus. It was too dark and too far away to tell for sure. On the left side of the road there was a drainage ditch and more scrub beyond that. The nearest streetlight was many miles away. At night the area was so deserted that anyone driving the road was alone. It probably was deserted in the daytime, too. I didn't even know where the road went, except that it was no where I wanted to be.

But tonight was different. Death drew a crowd. Up ahead of where I parked it looked like a crime scene always does. There were too many police cars and the flashing lights gave everything an eerie and disorienting look while not really illuminating anything. A half-dozen uniformed cops stood around doing nothing in particular. Somewhere in the distance I could hear someone talking to what probably was headquarters, with that peculiar hollow-sounding crackle that I never heard anywhere else.

There was an ambulance on the other end of the line of cars on the side of the road where I parked. The lights were off and the engine wasn't running. It didn't seem to be going anywhere anytime soon. Two EMT's stood next to the cab. One of them was smoking a cigarette. He finished it, dropped it on the asphalt, and ground it out with his sneaker.

A uniform cop with aviator glasses perched on a broken nose stepped in my way and put a hand none to gently on my shoulder.

"*Esta esla escena del crimen restringdo,*" he said.

I already knew it was a crime scene. I shrugged his hand off my shoulder, stuck my pointed finger under his nose, and barked, "Valencia, *pronto.*"

His eyes narrowed and he stepped back. Not sure what to make of me. I learned a long time ago that attitude gets you a long way in Mexico.

I reached into my pocket, pulled out my wallet and removed my magic card. Using his flashlight, the cop carefully read it. Before handing the card back, he sullenly looked me up and down to establish that he really was a tough guy despite having to give in this time.

"*Espera aqui,*" he ordered.

I waited, like he asked.

He motioned to another cop with his head. He didn't say anything, but it was a signal to keep an eye on me while he looked for Valencia. For all they knew, I was the murderer and I'd come back to gloat. He stepped off the shoulder of the road and walked down into the knee-high weeds. headed for the stand of cactus in the distance, where for the first time I saw flashlights bobbing around. From this far away they looked like fire-flies. Without seeming to do anything in particular, the cop he motioned to sidled in my direction, crossed his arms over his chest, leaned back against a patrol car and waited, watching with great vigilance.

My hero was back in a few minutes and motioned toward the distant lights.

"Over there," he said, making a waving motion with one hand.

It hadn't rained for a long time and the ground was hard and uneven. I'd left my flashlight in the Mustang so I had to force myself to walk slowly and carefully through the thigh-high weeds and over many ruts when what I really wanted to do was run like hell.

When I was a kid, probably thirteen, or so, a girl I knew had a party at her house. It was the most innocent thing in the world. Our idea of unbridled passion was slow dancing. A pal of mine had an argument with his girlfriend. Full of the hot frustration that comes so easily to young people, he stormed out of the house and walked out into the darkness.

After a while, he calmed down and started back to the party. Instead of staying on the street, he cut across a field. That was when the rattlesnake got him. Under the circumstances, it was asking too much of a kid to keep a cool head. He panicked and did exactly the wrong thing by running back to the house so that the venom pumped through his system. The father of the girl giving the party took him to the hospital, which was less than a mile away. He died the next morning.

Some people from the city went snake hunting in the field and killed two big rattlers. Ever since then, walking through an empty field in the dark was not my idea of a good time, especially considering what I was going to find at the end of this trip.

As I got closer, the figures I'd seen earlier became more distinct. Three cops with flashlights walked around in ever-increasing circles, while a couple of others were busy setting up a stand of halogen lights to illuminate the area. Then I saw two other men standing by a tall cactus staring at the ground. Valencia was one of them.

A uniformed cop came toward me with his hand raised, stumbling a little on the uneven ground.

"*Dejarlo pasar*," Valencia ordered. The cop stepped aside and let me pass.

I walked up beside Valencia and saw what they were staring at.

She was lying on her back with her chin tilted toward the sky. Her mouth was slightly open and her sightless eyes stared at the stars shining through the night. She was wearing workout clothes - white socks, athletic shoes, a black spandex outfit that came down to just above her knees, and a bright red t-shirt.

It looked like her, but it wasn't, not really. The flesh had fallen back from her face so that it seemed sharper and more pointed than it did in life. And it wasn't as if she was just sleeping. Instead, it was as if someone attempted a failed reproduction of the real thing. They got all the details right but couldn't capture the life force that was Abby LaForge. Such a thing was impossible.

I looked at Valencia and he nodded. I knelt beside her. Even her tousled blonde hair seemed lifeless. No, this wasn't the woman I knew. She didn't exist anymore. Someone took her life away.

There was a heavy feeling in my chest. My throat

seemed to close and I couldn't get a deep breath. An ant crawled along her cheek. Gently, I reached out and brushed it off. It was the least I could do for someone I'd failed so badly.

After a moment, I stood up. Valencia jerked his head to motion us away from the body.

We walked far enough to be out of earshot and stopped, looking out at the darkness.

"Are you all right?" he asked.

"Yeah," I said. "But it's different when it's somebody you know."

"Every time is different," he said. "But knowing does make it worse."

I took a deep breath and slowly let it out.

"Especially this time," I said. "There was something about her. I dunno ..."

I shook my head, wanting to clear away the heaviness of it. I had the urge to run away and hide like a little boy, but it had been a long time since I was a little boy.

"What do you know?" I asked.

"She was shot in the back of the head by a small caliber weapon. Almost certainly killed somewhere else and brought here."

"Yeah, it's not very likely that she had the sudden urge to take a hike in the woods far from home in her workout clothes and just happened to run into somebody who put a bullet in her head," I agreed. "Who found her?"

Valencia pointed his chin to somewhere in the far distance.

"An old man who lives in an even older house on the other side of the woods was walking his dog before he went to bed. He usually goes in the opposite direction and can't explain why he came this way. Perhaps it was just something different in an old man's life. The dog ran over here, began barking, and wouldn't come back. The old man had a flashlight and walked over to see what was wrong. It took a long time. The ground is rough and he is very old. He found the dog nosing at the body. He dragged the dog away, stumbled home, and called us. Once I got here and heard his story I had a man take him to the hospital. The effort exhausted him and the body frightened him."

I looked back at the road and the cars with all their flashing lights.

"Drew a helluva crowd," I said.

"My men knew who it was even before I arrived," he said.

"How?"

"She had some identification in a little thing strapped to her ankle. She probably wore it when she went to work out so she didn't have to carry a purse. Many women do that, I understand."

"Any idea when she was shot?"

"It's been some time, but hours, not days," he said. "We will know more later."

"How long has she been here?"

"We don't know."

"Is her car around?"

"We haven't found it so far. It's certainly not within a mile of here. My thought is that she was killed elsewhere, the killer drove her here, carried her from the car, and dumped the body."

"Unless he drove through the field to get here he must be a strong guy. That's a pretty long way to carry a body."

"Unless there was more than one. It doesn't have to be a man. And any four-wheel-drive vehicle could get out here from the road."

"Yeah," I said. "And if they drove her out here it's probably too dry to find tracks in the dirt. Did the old guy who found her hear anything?"

"No," Valencia said. "And I would not expect him to. He lives perhaps three-quarters of a mile away. Every night of his life he is in his old house with the television on. There is no one on this road day or night, at least not so it matters, and there is no one in this field. You could do anything here and no one would be around to see or hear it. If it hadn't been for the dog it would have been a long time before the body was found. Months or maybe even years. We were lucky."

"Yeah, weren't we though," I said.

"Are you sure that you're all right?"

"I'm sure," I said, working hard to stay focused. "You said she was shot by a small caliber weapon."

"Yes. We will know the caliber later."

"Small, like Jimmy Hopper and the bullets left in the mail box?"

"Yes, like that."

"Where's Jeff?" I asked.

"He is on the way."

"Anything else?"

"Not yet. Late tomorrow" - Valencia looked at his watch - "or rather late today, we will know more. Why don't I call you? Perhaps you shouldn't be seen here when the husband arrives. He might not like it if he finds out that I called you first."

"I'm the least of his problems," I said. "You know, I saw Jeff earlier today. He said Abby left to workout while he was still asleep. That was her routine. She did it several times a week, regular as can be."

"Did he say anything else?"

"Nothing that matters." I gave him a quick recap of

the conversation so Valencia could compare the stories when he talked to LaForge. Standard procedure.

"I am going to try to keep this quiet for a while," Valencia said. "From what you told Garcia, this man Bergman is our prime suspect. But I am not going to bring him in yet."

"Why not?" I said. "I know Mexican law. You don't have to arrest him to keep him."

"Once I did that I could not keep it quiet," he said. "With the new facility, the many new jobs, and all it means to Cabo San Lucas, plus the promise of more elsewhere in Mexico, putting the number two man under suspicion of murder would create a media orgy in two countries. We will bring him in when we need to. But on the chance that he didn't do it I don't want whoever might have done it to know that we found the body. Maybe they will make a mistake. If it's Bergman, we will watch him and maybe he'll do something to reveal himself. It can't hurt to keep it quiet and it might help."

"A lot of people know already," I said. "It's gonna be hard to keep it a secret."

"Not forever, just for a little while," he said. "Let's see what happens. Once we get a better idea when she was shot can you quietly check with someone to see if they know where Bergman was at that time? An official inquiry from us would draw attention."

"Sure," I said, thinking that I'd call Linda Giordano.

I didn't tell him about the photographs I'd seen at Bergman's place. I wasn't sure why I held it back. I just did.

"What are you gonna do about ... Abby?" I asked. It was hard to say her name. Calling her "the victim," as the police usually did, kept it clinical.

"With her husband's permission, I will keep her under an anonymous name. How do you put it?"

"A Mexican Jane Doe?"

Valencia nodded. "For a while."

We walked back to the road. Any chance of snakes had been pushed out of my head.

There weren't as many police cars parked on the road now. We were far enough from the city lights that the sky seemed full of stars, the way it often did in Cabo. Neither of us said anything. There was nothing to say. The EMTs were gone. The ambulance was replaced by the white coroner's van. I pushed away the thought of an autopsy. What I'd seen out there wasn't Abby anyway.

I'd just slid behind the wheel of the Mustang when an unmarked police car drove up and parked on the other side of the road about twenty yards ahead of me. Jeff LaForge jumped out of the front seat without closing the door.

A cop walked up to stop him, but LaForge brushed away his hand.

"Where's my wife?" There was a panicky, choking sound in his voice. "Where's Abby?"

Valencia came up from behind, got a grip on LaForge's arm just above the elbow and guided him to the side of the road. With Valencia controlling him, LaForge seemed to stumble as if he'd lost some of his motor skills.

I'd seen enough. I started the Mustang, backed up, made a U turn and drove away as I rolled down the window. I wanted the cool night air on my face.

I hadn't gone far when I gripped the top of the steering wheel as hard as I could with both hands, threw back my head and screamed into the night. I bellowed with everything I had from deep inside. I screamed and screamed and screamed until my voice was hoarse and I couldn't do it anymore.

When I got home, I took off my clothes and crawled in

bed. Sleep did not come for a long time. But finally, just before dawn, it did.

Hours later, in that twilight stage before I was fully awake, I was sure that I'd dreamed everything from last night and when I woke up I'd find that nothing had happened and life would be as it was. But even then, I knew that I was wrong.

CHAPTER 35

"SHE WAS SHOT behind the left ear with a twenty two caliber weapon."

Valencia got his information sooner than I expected, mostly because he kept his people up all night getting it. We met for breakfast at a small palapa restaurant near the police station. Valencia had his usual nothing; black coffee and half slice of toast with nothing on it. I was surprisingly hungry and wolfed down an omelet slathered in guacamole and salsa, well done hash browns, and a tortilla, washing it down with orange juice and three cups of coffee.

"Whoever did it was right next to her," Valencia said. "She was shot at least twenty four hours before we found the body. The manager of her workout facility said that she didn't show up that morning. According to the register, she rarely misses a workout when she's in Cabo San Lucas."

"That's what Jeff said," I agreed. "So for somebody stalking her, being so predictable made it easy. She had her workout clothes on, so that meant they got her after she left the house but before she got to her club."

It was so obvious that Valencia didn't bother to agree.

Despite my hunger, I felt a little woozy and vaguely disoriented, like I was hung over without having had anything to drink. Some of it was lack of sleep, but most of it wasn't. I should have called my psychiatrist but I didn't want to. I was tired of trying to find meaning in every little word and gesture and trying to interpret things that maybe didn't mean anything in the first place. After years of therapy I wasn't sure that I was any better off than I was when I started. I was sick of me.

"Anybody at the club see her car?" I asked.

"No, but they weren't looking for it," he said. "Most of the people who work out that early are still half asleep when they get there. We found her car, a late model Jeep SUV, in a *mercado* parking lot not far away, but it doesn't mean that's where she was shot. There wasn't any blood in the Jeep, but the head wound didn't bleed very much, not with a twenty two. So perhaps she wasn't shot in the car?"

"Prints?"

Valencia would have told me if they'd found any, but I asked anyway.

"Just what you would expect," he said. "Hers and his. Nothing unusual."

I took a sip of my coffee. A gray-haired waitress with bowed legs walked by with a coffee pot and asked if I wanted a refill.

I shook my head. "No *gracias*."

The waitress was too old to be doing what she was doing. By the time you get to your sixties, life ought to be easier than waiting tables in a joint like this. She probably was somebody's grandmother and never thought her life would turn out the way it did. I felt bad about turning down her coffee.

"There are two other interesting details," Valencia said.

"What?"

"There were red fibers on her clothes."

"Red fibers?"

"Probably from a rug. I sent them away to be analyzed."

"You think somebody wrapped her body in a rug before they dumped her in the field?"

"It is a way of concealment and made the body easier to carry. Or perhaps she wore her workout clothes more than once and just happened to toss them on a red rug after the first time?"

"No," I said, "I don't think so. Abby was too fastidious for that. She'd never wear the same workout clothes twice without washing them."

"And she was pregnant," he said.

As I sat there with my mouth open, Valencia added that LaForge agreed not to tell anyone about his wife's death. If anyone asks, he'll say she visiting a friend in the states.

"He is also going to take some time off, but he will stay in Cabo San Lucas," Valencia said.

"She was pregnant? Are you sure?"

"As sure as modern science can be."

"Does LaForge know?" I asked.

"I don't know." Valencia frowned, surprised at the question. "I didn't learn about it until after I talked to him. Why wouldn't he know?"

I regretted the question. "Hell, I'm not even sure why I asked. I'm babbling. Still can't believe it, I guess. How pregnant was she?"

"Not very. Just enough to detect."

Valencia said the department had a tail on Bergman, so I could call my man off.

"You spotted him?" I asked.

He shot me a look over his coffee cup.

"Do you think we are amateurs? And we do talk, Garcia and me. It is, after all, an ongoing investigation and he is my nephew. He was good, however. The boy is very good."

In all the activity, I'd forgotten that Garcia was Valencia's nephew.

We got up to leave. As usual when dining with Valencia in Cabo, there was no check.

"I'll leave the tip," I said.

Valencia's eyes widened when he saw the size of the tip. It was more than the bill.

"You must have liked breakfast very much."

"I feel sorry for the waitress," I explained. "She's too old to be doing what she's doing."

I stood beside the Mustang, folded my arms on the closed roof and rested my chin on my hands. It was a beautiful morning, all blue sky and soft breezes. I didn't give a damn.

Something about the red fibers nagged at me, but I couldn't pin it down. Besides, another fact loomed much larger. During those moments in the distant past when we pretended to get along, LaForge and I used to joke about how, despite what they claim, it's definitely not painless. In fact, it hurts like hell for a while: We'd both had vasectomies.

That was why I asked Valencia if LaForge knew about his wife's pregnancy. Whoever the father of Abby LaForge's baby was, it wasn't her husband. There were a couple of pretty good candidates. Despite what Abby said, one was Jimmy Hopper. The other was Mort Bergman. I couldn't talk to Hopper, but I sure as hell intended to talk to Bergman.

CHAPTER 36

As soon as I got back to my office, I called Garcia and told him he could stop tailing Bergman.

"Good," he said. "When I saw the *policia* watching, too, I felt a little silly. What now? Please don't say more gardening."

"I don't know," I confessed. "I'll get back to you."

I wished that Dina was here so I could talk to her. She always helped clarify my thoughts, assuming I had any. She felt the same way when she had a problem.

I drove to Bergman's condo late that night. I spotted Valencia's man right away, lazing away the hours in an unmarked car down the street. He was easy to spot. Nothing looks like an unmarked police car except an unmarked police car, even in Mexico. Besides, surveillance usually is easy to find if you already know it's there. He was right where I would have been: About halfway down the block in front of the condo, looking as bored as he probably was. The fact that he was there told me that Bergman was home.

Valencia wouldn't like what I was about to do, but I didn't care. The memory of Abby LaForge with her dead eyes looking up at the sky was too vivid.

I was certain that the surveillance wasn't a two-man job, at least not two men at the same time. For one thing, the Cabo police department couldn't afford it. But I still parked the Mustang several blocks away and carefully canvassed the neighborhood on foot to make sure.

I was wearing black jeans, a black pullover shirt, my dark brown Rockports, and the Sig in a holster at the small of my back. Purists would be appalled with the way the black jeans and brown shoes clashed. If what I was about to do went bad I'd look damned unfashionable in jail, where Valencia wouldn't hesitate to put me if I put him in a bad mood.

I walked up the alley in back of the condo, carefully avoiding any light shining through neighboring windows on the way. After a final look around to make sure no one was watching, I put my palms on top of the stucco wall in back of Bergman's place and easily climbed over. I didn't want to open the gate and risk the ugly scraping sound again. It wouldn't do to go over the wall in the daylight, but in a night as dark as this one I was okay. With what I had on, the darkness, and the late hour, I was confident that no one saw me.

Bergman's ground floor windows were open. I looked in the kitchen window and didn't see anything, although I couldn't see the whole area. At the same time, I heard the faint sound of water running through the pipes. There was too much of it to be the bathroom sink. He must be taking a shower upstairs.

I went up the steps to the back door. I tried the door, but it was locked. I'd left my burglary kit in the car. After another glance around, I muttered, "Screw it!" I took a step back, put my shoulder down, and rammed the door as hard as I could.

The door jam, lock, and part of the door splintered apart. To me it sounded louder than thunder, but it prob-

ably wasn't that bad. I paused just inside the door to reas-
sure myself that Bergman still had the shower going. He
did. It's hard to hear anything while you're taking
shower. If any of the neighbors heard me bull through the
door they probably didn't think anything of it. It was just
another random sound from somewhere out in the darkness. The scrape of a sagging gate sounds like what it is,
especially if you've heard it before. What I'd done was
harder to place. Valencia's watcher out front was too far
away to hear anything.

I closed the broken door and braced it with a dining
room chair to keep it from sagging open. The front
curtains were pulled and no lights were on downstairs,
so the cop outside couldn't see inside. From his position
down the street, he couldn't see anything inside even if
the curtains were open. I moved over to the staircase and
listened. Bergman was still in the shower. Cleanliness is
my friend.

Moving as quietly but as quickly as possible, I went
up the stairs two at a time, stopping in a crouch at the top
of the stairs. The bedroom light was on and the shower
had come to an end. I could hear Bergman humming
tunelessly in the bathroom off the master bedroom.

I moved down the hall, passing the door to the office
where Bergman kept his Abby LaForge photo collection. I
risked a quick peek into the master bedroom. Bergman
had those curtains drawn, too.

I stepped into the room just as he walked out of the
bathroom rubbing his head with a towel. He was wearing
a pair of dark blue boxer shorts. He had a better build
than I thought he did. His clothes were always so shape-
less that it was impossible to tell if he was in good condition. There wasn't any fat on him and his shoulders were
surprisingly broad. He probably got that from swimming
all those laps in the condo pool.

He gasped when he saw me, stepped back, and bumped into the lamp on his bedside table. It would have fallen to the floor, but he involuntarily steadied it with one hand.

"Ethan? What the hell are you doing here? How'd you get in?"

"Get some clothes on," I said. "We're going to have a talk."

"What?"

"I said get dressed! Now!"

"What are you …?"

Before I knew it, I'd covered the distance between us and had my right hand around his throat. I shoved him back against the wall. He was too surprised to resist. There wasn't much he could have done even if he tried.

"I know about your little photo collection in the other room," I said. "I know you had an affair with Abby LaForge. I know you had me followed. I know you sent three guys after me. I know a lot of things you don't want me to know. And I know if you don't get dressed right now I'm going to beat on you until you tell me what I want to know and I'm gonna enjoy every minute of it."

Then I had a better thought.

"On the other hand, why bother with clothes?" I said. "Come along."

Like an old-fashioned grade-school teacher, I grabbed his ear between my index finger and thumb and twisted hard.

"Hey! That hurts!" He clutched at my hand with both of his, but I was stronger than he was and had a good hard grip on his ear. With Bergman staggering along behind me, I yanked him across the bedroom, out the door, down the hall, and into the office. I flipped on the wall light switch with one hand and guided him into the desk chair with my other hand still twisting his ear.

Being naked – or almost naked – makes you feel vulnerable, which was how I wanted Bergman to feel. It also makes the other person feel more powerful. Kinky. Someone once told me that the way to overcome a fear of public speaking was to imagine everyone in the audience stark naked. The thought almost killed my power of speech.

The bright overhead light emphasized Bergman's pale skin. How could a guy swim laps in an outdoor pool in Mexico and not get a tan? His thinning hair was in disarray from the shower and he looked cold and uncomfortable, probably because he was.

"What are you *doing?*" Rubbing his ear, Bergman started to rise out of the chair, which I thwarted by shoving him back with one hand.

He tried it again, and again he was thwarted. He gave up and tried looking defiant instead. That didn't work either. It's a hard look to pull off when you're only wearing underwear, your wet hair is pointing every which way, and you've just been dragged around by the ear.

"Ethan, what do you want? Goddamit! What's this all about?"

"I want to know about you and Abby, *everything* about you and Abby."

I put my hands on my knees and loomed over him like I was about to belt him in the mouth. I thought I was faking, but I wasn't sure. I really wanted to belt him. The fact that he looked so ridiculous only made it more tempting. This pipsqueak wasn't worth all the trouble he'd caused.

Mort Bergman was a man I used to like, but now I knew him for what he was. Like Valencia, I didn't know for sure that he'd killed Abby, although I thought he probably did. But if he did, I wanted to hear it from him myself, not second hand. Besides, there were a lot of other things I didn't know and he was going to tell me or I probably *would* start beating on him.

I leaned forward so that my face was uncomfortably close to his. He tried pulling back, but he didn't have anywhere to go.

"If you leave anything out, I'll know it. Abby's dead and the police think you killed her. As a matter of fact, so do I."

"Abby ... Abby's ... Abby's dead?"

I stood up, grabbed a handful of what was left of his hair and jerked his head back.

"Stop the bullshit," I snarled.

I let go of his hair. Bergman glanced over at the photographs and then looked down at his bare feet, covering his eyes with one hand.

After a while, he began to talk.

CHAPTER 37

HE TALKED FOR ALMOST AN HOUR. In the end, I think he was relieved to get it all out.

Several times he asked if he could put some clothes on, but I had a good thing going and didn't want to screw it up. In an effort to keep warm, he brought his knees up to his chest and wrapped his arms around his legs. It made him look even more pathetic than he already did. Too bad.

He confirmed a lot of what I already knew. Yes, he had an off and on affair with Abby. Yes, that was the reason his marriage broke up. Yes, he was obsessed with her. He had it bad, knew it, and there wasn't anything he could do about it. That's the nature of obsession. The way she sometimes ridiculed him only added to it. He didn't enjoy being abused, except by Abby LaForge.

From time to time, his eyes involuntarily wandered over to the photographs above the desk.

"I used to watch her and wonder what it'd be like to make love to a woman like that," he said. "Jane wasn't much when it came to sex. She never seemed interested."

His back was starting to hurt from the awkward position. He leaned forward in the chair, put his elbows on his bony knees and cradled his head in his hands.

"I don't know," he said, talking to the floor. "Maybe Jane just didn't like it with me. Maybe it would have been different with someone else. Even when we were first married, she acted like it was an obligation when we did it at all, like it was her wifely duty, or something. At least once in my life, I wanted to be with someone who enjoyed it. And I could tell Abby did. Anybody could. You know what she was like."

"Christ, I hope to hell it was worth it," I muttered.

He jerked upright. All of a sudden his face was shining and eager. He'd forgotten that Abby was dead. He'd forgotten that he was sitting in his boxer shorts while I threatened him. He'd forgotten all but one thing.

"You can't imagine," he said. "I never knew it could be like that."

I decided to take a shot and see if I hit anything.

"When did you find out she was pregnant?"

The look on his face told me that he was surprised that I knew.

"It wasn't long before Jeff started getting the threats," he said. "When I found out, I told her, 'Well, at least we can get married now.' I mean, Jeff'll know it's not his. He can't have children and he couldn't handle it if his wife had somebody else's baby. Not many men, could, I guess. But Abby just laughed at me. She said she needed me to get pregnant and that's all she needed me for. She'd take care of everything else by herself."

I couldn't believe what I just heard.

"Are you telling me that Abby *wanted* to have a baby?"

Bergman's head bobbed up and down. "I couldn't believe it either. I mean, it never even occurred to me. I never used a rubber, or anything. She said it wasn't necessary so I assumed she was taking the pill, or something."

"The way things turned out, it didn't really matter, did it?" I said.

Reminded that Abby was dead, Bergman seemed to shrink in on himself until he looked even smaller and more pale than before. He sure as hell didn't look like someone Abby LaForge might cut out of the herd.

"You know, that was when she said the nicest thing she ever said to me. She said, 'You're not a bad guy. You're smart, you're kind, and you'd even be pretty good looking if you knew how to dress and take care of yourself. It's too bad you're so weak.' Actually she said, 'fucking weak.'"

Jesus! If that was the nicest thing Abby LaForge she ever told Mort Bergman, it must have been a hell of a relationship. But I knew that already.

Bergman resolutely denied having anything to do with threatening Jeff or Abby. Chin quivering, he denied killing Abby, too.

He was right on the edge. I had to be careful not to press too hard or he wouldn't be any use to me.

He asked when Abby was killed. I told him and asked where he was during the time Valencia said she probably was killed.

He hesitated. "Working, mostly, I guess. The rest I can't … ."

Which was when I hit him, a long back-handed slap across the face that bloodied his nose. It didn't feel as good as I thought it would, not when what I really wanted to do was beat him until he was a bloody mush.

It turned out that he went to a Cabo whore house after leaving the office and stayed the rest of the night. Until I hit him, he was too embarrassed to say it.

"After Abby, I was getting … I was … ."

"Horny," I said.

Bergman slumped over in the chair so that his head was almost to his knees and started crying, his back rippling with each sob.

I didn't care about that either. I was focused on the fact that his alibi was so pathetic that it had to be true. Besides, Garcia could confirm it, too. He hadn't mentioned it, but why would he? A single man who wants to get laid is not exactly unusual in Cabo San Lucas, or anywhere. We were looking for a guy making threats and acting suspicious, not a guy paying money to get screwed.

"I did send those guys after you," he admitted, straightening up as he wiped the tears from his red-splotched face. "Or anyway I paid some guy to send them after you. I'm sorry about that. I really am."

"Why did you do it?"

"I wanted to make you stop poking into everything," he said. "I was afraid you'd find out about Abby and me. They were supposed to break your leg so you'd have to give up. When that didn't work, I had you followed. I had to know what you were up to. But the guy just disappeared. You see, Abby didn't want it to get out that we were together. Jane knew about it 'cause she saw us at a hotel, but we knew she wouldn't say anything. All she did was crawl into a bottle. Abby was afraid that Jeff might do something to me if he found out. I mean, at the very least he could ruin my career. I guess that doesn't matter now, does it? I've been so stupid. I've never done anything like this before. It's like I was out of control."

"You're wrong about Jane," I said. "She was always willing to talk. It's just that nobody bothered to ask her. It's like she never existed."

Bergman didn't get it. The man was dry. He wasn't even scared anymore. There was nothing left. Hearing that Abby was dead and the humiliation of being forced to talk about all that happened between them took his heart away.

But there were a few more things I wanted to know.

"What makes you think that you were the only one?" I asked. "For all you know, she had men lined up from here to Seattle. A lot of people thought that Abby and Jimmy Hopper …."

He shook his head. It was a violent motion full of emphatic denial.

"You don't get it," he said. "I didn't figure it out until toward the end myself. Abby wasn't just screwing around. She wanted to have a baby. Looking back, I figured out that we only did it when she thought she had the best chance of getting pregnant. All the stops and starts made me crazy. I wanted to be with her all the time. Until you showed up I followed her whenever I could, even when she was with Jeff. Sometimes I'd sneak up to a window at their house. I stopped because I was afraid you'd catch me." He made a weak gesture at the photographs. That's how I got … all those. If she was with somebody else I would have known about it. She and Jimmy were never more than friends."

"Why you?" I asked.

"What do you mean?"

"Abby could have had her pick," I said. "So why you?"

"I don't know." He shook his head. "I almost asked a couple of times, but I was afraid to. I wanted to know, but I didn't want to ruin it. You know what I mean?"

I felt like I could hear my own pulse. Bergman looked exhausted. My adrenaline rush had long since passed and I was tired, too.

"What about the threats?" I asked.

"I told you before, I don't know anything about

those," he said. "I didn't have anything to do with it. Ethan, you've gotta believe me. Why would I lie now?"

Pleading, he looked up at me. Sitting in his underwear under the harsh overhead light he seemed grotesque, like the Gollum in "Lord of the Rings."

"I'm not a bad man," he said, "Really, I'm not. Jesus, I can't believe this is happening."

He buried his faces in his hands and began to cry again.

To my surprise, I believed him. Mort Bergman wasn't a bad man. He was pathetic, he was ridiculous, and he was in so far over his head he couldn't find a way out even if he knew which way to go, but he wasn't a bad man. He just didn't know how to live his own life. He never did. When somebody – Abby LaForge – threw him a scrap, he took it and begged for more.

I left him there. I told him that the police would come sooner or later, but as long as his alibi held up he'd be okay. I told him that I wouldn't say anything about sending the three guys after me and suggested that he might want to get rid of the photographs of Abby before the cops showed up.

He stood up then. He was so cold there were goose pimples on his arms and legs. He folded his arms and hunched his shoulders in a feeble attempt to get warm.

"Ethan, please tell me, how did Abby die?"

"Somebody shot her in the back of the head and dumped her body in a field," I said.

"I'm sorry," he said, staring down at his feet. "God, I'm so sorry."

"Oh, shut the fuck up," I said.

CHAPTER 38

I WAS SIPPING a cup of coffee on the patio in back of my house overlooking the bright blue water of the Gulf of California when Valencia came blowing in the way a tornado enters a trailer park. Garcia followed along behind like a puppy following a mastiff. Everything about the younger man said that he was not happy to be here.

Valencia didn't bother to sit down. He leaned forward, put his fists on the patio table, and glared at me, poised like a snake about to strike.

"I should throw you in jail right now," he growled.

I saluted him with my coffee, took a sip, and put it on the table.

"Top of the morning to you, too," I said. "Coffee?"

"For once, don't be a *culo inteligente*," he snapped. "I'm tired of your act."

The tremor in Valencia's voice told me that he was holding his temper, but just barely. He obviously thought I was a lot worse than the smart ass he called me.

"I trusted you. I let you in on the investigation and you ran your own little operation, as usual. You kept information from me, you talked to our suspect before we did, despite what I told you I wanted, and I am sure that you hid evidence, too. How many years in jail do you think all that is worth?"

The more Valencia talked the angrier he got. With one long motion of his arm, he swept everything off the table, including my coffee, an oil lamp, and the newspaper I hadn't gotten around to reading. The lamp and coffee cup shattered when they hit the *Saltillo* tile and black coffee and cold oil flew everywhere.

Aside from the mess, the only thing Valencia accomplished was to make me as angry as he was. I jumped to my feet so that we were nose to nose over the table, except my nose was higher than his. It wasn't much of an advantage, but it helped.

"Put a cork in it, *jefe*," I said, with all the sarcasm I could muster. "How can I screw up your investigation when you're doing such a good job of it to yourself? You and your crack squad of low rent crime busters haven't turned up jack. From what I've seen on this case you couldn't find your ass with both hands and a flashlight. Maybe you should stick to handling boozed up tourists? That's about all your department seems to be worth. And if you're gonna try to haul me anywhere you'd better get help. By the way, Mort Bergman didn't kill Abby LaForge. He has a solid alibi. It's pretty pathetic, but it's solid."

While I was ranting, I stepped around the table so that Valencia and I didn't have to lean in to be face to face. He looked like he might explode. I probably looked a little piqued myself. I didn't know if I could take him, if it came to that, but I didn't know if he could take me either.

"I don't care if Bergman has a note from the *puta* mother," Valencia growled. "This isn't about him. It's about you. I'll say it so that even you can understand: You've never done anything but fuck up your whole life and now you're fucking up my investigation."

We were on the edge of I don't know what, but before we fell off that edge Garcia wedged himself between us. He was surprisingly strong for such a roly-poly guy.

"This is *not* getting us anywhere," he said, the youngest among us showing the only maturity in sight. "Why don't you two stop oozing *machismo* for a minute and sit down? Do you wanna try and solve this thing, or stand around and shout at each other like a couple of *ninos*?"

As the three of us posed in an awkward tableau, my heart was pounding so hard they probably could hear it all the way down at Cabo Wabo.

Valencia's chest rose and fell as he took a deep breath and let it out with a hiss, trying to regain the control he'd lost, something I'd never seen him do.

"You were wrong, you know that, don't you?" he said.

His eyes were still hot, but his voice had less anger than it did a moment ago.

"No, I don't know that," I said. "I don't work for you and I don't have to follow your rules, as long as I don't break any laws. And you damn well know *that*!"

Valencia seized the heavy wrought iron table and sent it sailing across the patio as if it was made of balsa wood. He took a step closer and we both prepared to go at it.

"Stop it! Both of you! Sit down! Now!"

Garcia's voice cut through the fog in my head like a laser. Like two chastised children, we thumped down in the patio chairs, with an empty space between us where the table used to be. Suddenly the anger was gone and I felt almost as silly as I'd been acting. Judging by embarrassment shading Valencia's eyes, he felt the same way. If there had been any dirt on the tiles, we probably would have scuffed our toes in it.

After letting us stew in our own idiocy for a moment, Garcia said, "That's much better. Ethan, why don't you explain what happened between you and Bergman. When the *policia* brought him in for questioning this morning, he said you practically spent the night with him."

I told them most, but not all, of what Bergman said. I needed to think about some things before I went any further. If I told Valencia everything, any leverage I had would disappear. I was taking a chance because it was possible that Bergman told them everything he told me. But, then again, maybe he didn't.

"His alibi is easy to check," I suggested.

"We already know," Valencia said. "The place is well known." He nodded at Garcia. "This man saw him go in. We confirmed that he stayed long enough to back it up."

"Maybe I should have said something," Garcia admitted. "But I figured the guy went out and got laid, so what? As long as he was doing that, he wasn't doing anything else."

"It looks like you two had a busy morning," I said. "What brought on all the sudden activity? I though you were gonna keep it quiet."

"Word got out about the LaForge murder," Valencia said. "You were right. Too many people knew. I couldn't hold it for as long as I wanted. We had to confront Bergman, which was when we found out that you were already there."

"And now the only suspect is in the clear," I said. "He didn't do it and we know it, so it's back to square one. Plus, we've still got nothing on the threats, not to mention Hopper's murder."

"Unless we can prove that they were linked, I don't care about Hopper's murder," Valencia said.

"I do," I said.

"I don't care about that either," he said.

After another long silence, young Garcia piped up again.

"The only thing we've got on Bergman is the three men he sent after you."

"He admitted that?" I asked.

"Yes, and he told us that he told you, too," Valencia said. He turned to Garcia. "And you will shut up. You are not part of any 'we' here. You have said enough. Do you understand?"

Looking as young as he was, Garcia stared hard at the ground. I felt sorry for the kid. Valencia was just reacting to the way he'd been scolded earlier.

"We saw his photo collection, too," Valencia continued. "He said that you told him to get rid of it before we got there. It seems that he couldn't bring himself to do it."

"I must have forgotten that part," I shrugged. "It was a long night."

"Did you forget anything else?" asked Valencia, who still was not the happiest man on the patio. "Good work on breaking in through the back door, by the way. Subtle, as usual."

"Whatever I said, would you believe me?"

"No," Valencia replied. "Right now, I wouldn't believe you if you said the sun was out."

I shrugged. "Then why should I say anything?"

There was another one of those clumsy silences while everybody waited for somebody else to get us out of this mess.

"Have you told Jeff LaForge the secret's out?" I asked

"Yes, we did that this morning, too."

"How'd he take it?"

"It was hard to tell," Valencia admitted. "I don't think the man ever stops posing. He acts like he thinks he should act and he has been doing it for so long that it's automatic by now. I think he's one of those people who wouldn't know a genuine human feeling if it sat on his lap."

"That's our Jeff," I said "All the world's a stage and we are his supporting players."

"Tell me, how are you supposed to act when your wife gets shot in the head and dumped in a field like garbage?" Garcia asked, breaking Valencia's order of silence.

I jumped in before Valencia could get on the boy's case again.

"Good point. He's dealing with it in his own way, I guess, like anybody would."

Valencia stared at me for a long time. He turned to Garcia and jerked his head as a command to leave.

"I don't know if you're holding back information," he said, stopping at the edge of the patio for one last volley. "Considering that you are very good at being a pain in the *cula,* I wouldn't be surprised if you were. I don't suppose it would do any good to ask you to let us know if you find anything? You know how it goes, keep us informed, the way it's supposed to work. I can make your life here a lot harder than it is and you know it."

"You just said that you don't believe me," I said. "What would be the point?"

"You could always try," he said. "I'm easy."

"Right,' I said. "Easy like a Doberman."

Valencia didn't laugh. "No more playing cowboy." The hard look in his dark eyes gave special meaning to the words.

As they left, I called out, "You owe me one oil lamp and one cup of expertly brewed coffee."

Without turning around, Valencia raised his right hand and waved his middle finger high.

So immature. Always trying to have the last word.

Before they rounded the corner of the house, I yelled to Garcia, "And kid, thanks for being the grown up."

CHAPTER 39

I GOT some paper towels and soaked them in water so I could clean the coffee off the patio before it stained the tile. The lamp was beyond repair so I stuffed the remains in the trash. I recovered the table and put it back in its place. The thing was heavy. Valencia's lean frame was a lot stronger than it looked.

I poured another cup of coffee to replace the one I never got to finish. I lied about the coffee. It wasn't expertly brewed. It was crap. Once again I had failed in the culinary arts. How the hell could I screw up coffee?

I leaned back in the chair and put both feet on the table. Dina used to call it my thinking pose. Most of the time it was just that, a pose, but nobody knew it but the two of us and she liked to tease me about it. If I achieved the perfect balance, sometimes I could even fall asleep.

There was none of that now. Something was bugging me and I didn't know what. It was out there somewhere just beyond my reach. What the hell was it?

I swung my legs off the table and sat bolt upright. I went inside to the trash, pulled out the remains of the lamp, fished through more trash, and found an advertisement from yesterday's mail suggesting that my life would be enhanced in grand and mysterious ways if I accepted a once in a lifetime offer to subscribe to a particular gun magazine at such a ridiculously low rate that the publisher might as well pay me.

Doing what I do put me on some unusual mailing lists, even in Mexico. Like most of my mail, I tossed the offer away without really looking at it. I didn't know why I remembered it, but when I did it triggered something in my head. I quickly strapped on the ankle holster and practically ran to the Mustang parked out front, climbed in, and barreled away.

Recalling the magazine offer somehow reminded me of what Jeff LaForge said about getting in some target practice. I was struck by the way he talked in the present tense about having a gun, as if he already owned one. Yet, when he first contacted me, he acted like he didn't know anything about guns.

There weren't many firing ranges in this part of the world. Most of the locals couldn't afford it and the tourists didn't care. In fact, as far as I knew there was only one at this end of the Baja Peninsula. I'd gone out there several times when we first moved to Cabo, but it had been a while. It was a primitive indoor-outdoor range a couple of miles off the highway corridor that linked Cabo San Lucas and San Jose del Cabo. I'd heard that the guy who owned it when we moved to Mexico had recently sold out.

After about twenty minutes of fast driving, I wheeled into the gravel parking lot and left the Mustang so that it faced the rectangular Quonset hut that was the firing range office. The day was already warm and the building's little window air conditioning unit was chattering away like it was about to have a nervous breakdown.

The old wooden door was badly warped and I had to give it a good push with my shoulder to get it open.

Nothing much had changed inside. It was still one of the ugliest rooms I'd ever seen. The floor was made up of cracked black-and-white linoleum squares, except that age had turned the white squares a kind of sickly yellow. The walls were cheap wood paneling that looked about two hundred years old. There was a gray metal desk on the other side of the room facing the door with a matching three-drawer file cabinet next to it. A water fountain stood in one corner. It was the metal stand-up kind with a pedal to get the water going that I always associated with public schools. A baby-poop green fake leather couch with cigarette burns on the arms and cushions was against the wall near the door. Three metal folding chairs haphazardly faced the couch, as if there had been some kind of meeting earlier today or last night.

Mine was the only car in the parking lot and the place didn't have any customers that I could see. I was about to go back outside and look around when I heard a toilet flush. Judging by the rattling sound, the plumbing was in the same shape as everything else. A door that I'd forgotten existed because it was covered with the same cheap wood paneling as the walls opened near the water fountain and a man stepped out in the process of zipping up his pants.

He saw me and took a quick step back into the bathroom, as if he'd like to try his entrance all over again and pretend that the first one didn't happen.

"Sorry," he said. "I didn't know anybody was here."

"Your secret's safe with me," I said.

"What secret?" he asked.

"Never mind," I said. "I was just kidding."

He looked like he was in his late forties or early fifties; a little shorter than me, maybe six feet tall, slim but not skinny. He wore Levis, hiking boots, and a white short-sleeved pullover shirt with lettering across the left side of the chest that advertised the shooting range. His sandy hair was neatly trimmed and gray at the temples. He was too fair-skinned to be out in the sun as much as he was and his nose was pink. His Bolle' sunglasses were tied to a cord that was hanging around his neck.

"What can I do for you?" he asked, his eyes moving down to my ankle. "I see you're wearing a piece. Come in for a little practice?"

"You're pretty observant," I said. "Pretty quick, too."

"I gotta be in this business," he said. "Whether somebody's carrying is the first thing I look for. Occasionally I get some yahoo in here who thinks he's Wyatt Earp. I gotta watch out for that kind of thing."

"How do you know I don't think I'm Wyatt Earp?" I asked.

"Maybe you do, but I doubt it," he explained. "I can tell when somebody's used to carrying. And most of the time only somebody who knows what they're doing bothers with an ankle rig."

"I think it makes me walk funny," I said.

"That's one reason why you don't see 'em that often," he grinned.

"You the owner now?"

"Yep, bought it from Jesus Ortega a while back."

"I used to come out sometimes when Jesus was here. It's been a while."

"He decided to give it up and sold out. Moved to someplace on the mainland toward the Gulf of Mexico side, I think. I'd served my twenty in the Marines. My Dad died and left me a little money. I used to come down here for the deep-sea fishing and thought I might want to live here someday. I wanted something to do and running this place turned out to be it. It's a good thing I don't need the money because it sure as hell doesn't make much."

When I nodded sympathetically, he asked, "You wanna hit the range?"

I hated to disappoint him. "Actually I'm just looking for some information." I handed him my business card. "I'm trying to find out if a certain person came here for lessons or practice."

"Got any other ID?" he asked. "Maybe something more official than a business card?"

I took out my wallet and showed him my magic card, along with my California PI license. He looked at both, looked at me, nodded, and handed them back.

"Thanks," he said. "Just tryin' to be careful. You know how it is."

"I understand. Now, about what I'm looking for …. "

"You want anything to drink?" he interrupted. "I've got iced tea, water, and soft drinks. No booze. Guns and alcohol make a bad mix."

I shook my head. He walked over to a waist-high refrigerator that was at least thirty years old and battered enough to fit in with the rest of the room, opened the door, and pulled out a bottle of Arizona Iced Tea. He twisted off the cap, dropped it in the trash, and waved the bottle in the direction of the folding chairs.

"Go ahead," he said. "Take a seat."

He reached out his empty hand and we shook.

"My name's Eckert," he said, "Mike Eckert."

"Ethan Cruickshank."

He sat behind the desk. I grabbed one of the metal folding chairs, lugged it over to the desk, turned it around, and sat backwards so that my forearms were resting on the back of the chair.

"So tell me about it," he asked. "Male or female? When would they have come in? Was it more than once? I guess it's not out of line for me to tell you if somebody was here."

I described Jeff LaForge. "My guess is that he probably came more than once, but I'm not sure. I don't even know if he was here at all."

Eckert took a sip of his iced tea and nodded approvingly.

"That's a pretty good description," he said. "I remember the guy."

"Yeah, and his wife's somebody you'd remember for sure," I said. "Abby's a hard woman to forget."

Eckert gave me a funny look over the top of his bottle as he took another drink.

"Something wrong?" I asked.

"Not a thing," he said. "Anyway, he was pretty eager. He claimed to have some experience from years ago, but it was pretty much like starting over."

"Was he any good?"

"It isn't that easy," he said. "You know that. But I got him to where he felt comfortable with the weapon. He wasn't as good as he thought he was. By his last lesson, he thought he was cooler than Elvis, but I see a lot of that."

I shifted a little in my chair and resisted the urge to blow on my hands to warm them up. For all its racket, the window air conditioner was an efficient little machine.

"You said 'the weapon,'" I asked. "One of yours, or did he have his own?"

"It was his, a little twenty two semi-automatic," he said.

"Did he tell you why he wanted lessons, or even felt that he needed a gun?"

"I don't know why he thought that he needed one, or how long he owned it, but my guess is that he bought what he had because it looked good."

"How do you mean?"

"It was a Beretta and that model looks like something out of 'Star Trek,'" he said. "You know, kind of futuristic. Guys almost always think it looks cool, like that'll make 'em a better shot, or something."

I already knew the answer, but I asked anyway.

"It could kill though?"

He raised his eyebrows at that. "Oh hell yes. You know that as well as I does. Like I said, it's a twenty two. At short range, it could kill you just as dead as anything else."

"Can you tell me when all this happened?" I asked. "When did he come in?"

Eckert tossed the empty ice tea bottle into the trash can beside his desk and began leafing through a desk calendar. Obviously, the man was a traditionalist. There was no keeping his appointments in a computer. In fact, he didn't seem to have a computer, at least not for business. After a little leafing through the calendar and some scribbling on a notepad, he tore off the page and pushed it across the desk. The four dates he'd written down were a perfect match with what I was already thinking.

"So what's going on?" he asked. "What's the deal with that 'can it kill?' question? You already knew the answer. If this guy comes back, should I tell him to get lost or call the *policia*?'"

"Sorry, but I can't say," I said. "And I'm pretty sure he won't be back."

"I've been straight with you," he protested.

"I know, and I appreciate it," I said. "But I can't say anything now. This has to do with a client.'"

I stood up to leave

"Thanks," I said. "You've been a big help."

"Anytime," he said. "And come back when you want a little practice."

"Jesus let me practice for free," I said. "We'd shoot

against each other for a bottle of scotch or a case of beer. Jesus always won."

Eckert looked dubious.

"That was pretty generous on his part," he said. "But maybe we can work *something* out."

"You said you don't need the money," I pointed out.

"Doesn't mean I don't *want* the money," he replied.

I walked out to the Mustang and got in. I started to crank the engine but something stopped me; the funny look he gave me when I mentioned Abby.

I went back into the Quonset hut.

Eckert was still at his desk. He'd picked up his cell phone and was about to make a call.

"Sorry to bother you again," I said. "But could you describe the woman who came in with him?"

"There wasn't a woman," he replied. "The LaForge guy was always by himself."

"Why didn't you say so?"

"You didn't ask."

CHAPTER 40

ON THE WAY back to the corridor, I turned off onto a dirt road I knew, drove up into the hills, found a sliver of shade under a pathetically parched tree, and looked out over the vista of beach and ocean a couple of miles away while I mulled over what I got out of Eckert and how it fit with everything else.

When I first talked to LaForge he said that he didn't know anything about guns. But later he all but bragged that he knew how to defend himself, just in case. He could have been talking about karate or kung fu or a magic incantation that turns people into toads, but I knew better. He was talking about a gun, which meant that he lied to me. The dates I got from Eckert confirmed it. Jeff was out at the gun range three times before he hired me, and then once more after that. He told me that Abby went with him, but, according to Eckert, she never did. Both Hopper and Abby were killed by shots from a twenty two in the back of the head at close range, the same caliber found in Jeff's mailbox, and the same caliber weapon he brought to the gun range.

Why would Jeff kill Jimmy Hopper? The answer was so easy I was embarrassed that I hadn't already thought of it. He assumed that Hopper was his wife's lover and the father of her unborn child. There were so many rumors floating around for so long that Hopper and Abby had something going on that Jeff must have heard them. Even if they weren't true, and by now I was pretty sure they weren't, I had no doubt that Jeff thought they were true.

The more I sat in the shade and thought about it the easier the rest of the pieces came together.

I knew that Jeff and Abby argued a lot. Were the arguments about her desire to have a child, or that she was pregnant with another man's child? Given that she was just barely pregnant when she was killed, it probably was both, first one, then the other. Somebody else was the stud on the farm and Jeff knew it. You don't call someone a fucking slut just because they want to have a baby.

Did Jeff know about Bergman and his wife? Almost certainly not at first. But what about later? I didn't know the answer to that one. Bergman wouldn't have been high on any list of possibilities. It could be that Jeff simply assumed that Hopper was the father and didn't think any further than that. I was sure that Jeff killed Hopper and Abby. If he'd known about Bergman he probably would have taken a run at him, too.

There are other ways to get pregnant. Why didn't Abby use one?

Maybe she wanted to know who the father was instead of getting pregnant by some stuff in a test tube, or however it's done? Or maybe there was some other reason? At this point, maybe it didn't matter?

So why didn't Jeff just get a divorce when he found out?

That was easy, too. Ego and money. It was okay for him to run around. He'd done that all his life. It was an entitlement that came with being Jeff LaForge. But his wife possessed no such entitlement. Other wives did, especially when the running around was done with him, but not *his* wife. The fact that Abby did it to have a child didn't matter. And maybe it shouldn't? The point is that everybody who knew Jeff well would know that the baby wasn't his and that would never do.

California being a community property state probably had something to do with it, too. Unless there was a prenuptial agreement, Abby would have gotten half of everything. Even if there was a prenup, the things get overturned fairly often. Jeff wouldn't have liked that either. In my experience, not many did.

Who would know if there was a prenup? Probably Linda Giordano. She seemed to know everything. I'd ask her later, but it probably wouldn't matter by then.

I had the feeling that Jane Bergman might fit in somewhere, but I didn't know where or how. She was a desperately unhappy woman who was bitter about losing her husband, drank too much, and hated Abby. I told Mort that despite what he thought Jane was always willing to talk, it's just that nobody bothered to ask her but me. What if I was wrong? Maybe she went to Jeff looking for sympathy or companionship from the other betrayed spouse? Or maybe she went to Jeff just to rat out Mort and Abby? I'd seen that happen many times in divorce cases. So did Jeff eventually learn that it was Mort all along? Or did Jeff even take Jane Bergman seriously, especially with all her boozing? I knew from experience that sometimes she didn't make a hell of a lot of sense. Either way, he could have used her somehow. In Jane's condition, she was easy prey for someone as slick and manipulative as Jeff LaForge. But if he used her, what did he use her for?

The logistics of the murder were fairly simple. After Jeff shot Abby, it was easy to take her body out to the boondocks and dump it. Like Valencia said, it was just luck that it was found so soon. Jeff probably planned to report that his wife was missing. The threats made it plausible.

And what about the threats?

It was so obvious now. There were no threats. They were all Jeff's work. It was the perfect distraction. Hopper's murder even helped. Nothing makes a threat seem serious like knowing the consequences of that threat are real. Jeff had all of us running around like crazy, looking for someone who wasn't there. Then, instead of killing Jeff LaForge, whoever made the threats killed his wife, who'd received a threat of her own. It was easy to explain the note left on Abby's SUV while Jeff was at Hopper's funeral, too. He probably paid somebody local a few bucks to watch Abby and leave it under her wiper. I doubted that whoever left the note it even knew what it was. As long as they got paid, why would they care? If some crazy gringo wants to spend his money in strange ways, that's his problem.

But why hire me when he already had the police looking for a phantom?

Another easy one. Hiring me showed how seriously he took the threats. He didn't think much of the Cabo police and made the case that the cops back in California had it in for him. Nobody really believed it but we were all convinced that Jeff believed it and that was all he needed. Under the circumstances, why not hire his own man, especially since it's somebody he already knows?

Of course, Jeff knew that I wouldn't find anything because there wasn't anything to find, at least not on the dead end trail I was following. And he assumed that he could outsmart us all and get away with it because that's the way he is. He's Jeff LaForge and he's smarter than everybody. Just ask him.

Red fibers!

Of course! It hit me like an electric shock. The first time I went to the LaForge house, one of the rooms I passed though had a big red rug with a Mexican design. The next time, it wasn't there, just bare tile. Jeff must have rolled Abby's body in it and then dumped it somewhere or destroyed it after he got rid of her.

So that was it. If I didn't have all the details exact, and I probably didn't, at least I had the broad strokes.

Part of me was angry that I hadn't put it together long before now, but I knew better than that. It's always easy to look back and see what you missed. At the time, it's a lot more complicated.

What now?

I should go to Valencia and tell him what I'd found and what I suspected, but I wasn't going to do that because I remembered Abby lying in the woods and Jimmy Hopper's widow trying to hold it together at the hospital.

But there was even more to it than that. I wanted to bring Jeff LaForge down. I wanted to do it myself, and I wanted him to know it was me who did it.

I didn't like the son of a bitch. I should have drowned him back when I had the chance.

CHAPTER 41

I DIDN'T HAVE much time. Abby's murder wasn't a secret anymore. It would take some time for the official report to work its way through the notoriously inefficient Mexican bureaucracy, but it would be public very soon.

I doubted that LaForge had talked to anybody. Not yet. His role right now was to play the grieving husband too overcome by sorrow to think of anything but his poor dead wife. If I knew Jeff LaForge, he was wearing custom tailored mourning clothes and practicing the right funeral poses in front of a mirror.

I left my shady spot, drove down from the hills, turned onto the highway corridor, and then turned onto a dirt road leading to the beach about a mile and a half from Jeff's upscale development. It was a popular spot for snorkelers and nobody would think anything of an unoccupied car. I'd decided to come in from the beach because I didn't want the guard at the entrance to alert Jeff that I was on the way.

I got out of the car and walked down the well-used path to the beach. There were a few snorkelers out in the water already, and a few more fussing with their equipment on the beach, but they paid me no attention.

I didn't have a plan. The best I could do was to impro-
vise my way through whatever might happen.

I trudged down the beach until I saw the LaForge
house in the distance, high on a promontory over the
beach. I stopped to call Garcia on my cell phone. When he
didn't answer, I left a message telling him a short version
of what I'd found out and where I was going.

Coming in from an angle that kept me out of sight of
the house, I carefully made my way up through the
scrub, rocks, and sand and peered in the garage window.
Jeff's Lexus was there. That didn't necessarily mean he
was home, but it was a high probability.

I quietly went around back by the pool and tried the
heavy sliding glass door. To my surprise, it was unlocked,
strange behavior for a man whose wife was murdered
and his own life threatened. I soundlessly opened the
door just enough so I could slide through, entered, and
moved toward the front of the house, carefully checking
each room as I passed.

I was in the living room and about to go upstairs
when I heard someone clear their throat behind me. I
turned around to see Jeff LaForge pointing a gun at my
midsection. Eckert's description was pretty accurate. The
Beretta did look like something out of a science fiction
movie.

"I saw you looking in the garage from upstairs and
walked down the outside stairs after you came in," he
said. "What the hell do you think you're doing?"

We stared at each other for a long time. The house was
silent except for our breathing.

"You know, don't you?" The way he said it wasn't a
question. He stared at me a little longer. "Yes, I believe
you do."

My gun was in my ankle holster. I didn't want to pull
it until I had to and now it was too late. I didn't know

how good he was with the Beretta but this was no time to find out. He'd already killed two people and wouldn't hesitate to make me number three.

"Tell me, Ethan, are you wearing a gun?" he asked.

He waited for an answer. When he didn't get one it made him angry.

"Talk, goddamit! Answer me!"

"Why bother when you're doing such a good job of answering your own questions," I sneered. "You always did like the sound of your own voice."

"Turn around asshole!"

When I did he stepped up and pressed the Beretta hard into the middle of my lower back, right at the spine. Using his left hand, he gave me the world's worst frisk, like something he learned watching television. But even that was enough to find my gun. He knelt, pulled it and backed away, with twelve feet or so between us.

"How'd you figure it out?" he asked. "I didn't make any mistakes. I'm sure of it."

As long as I kept him talking, he wasn't doing anything else. Like shooting me.

"Are you kidding?" I said. "You left so many loose ends I'm surprised you didn't trip and fall down. First you said you didn't know anything about guns, and then you did. I tracked you through the firing range. The guy there said you had a twenty two. Jimmy Hopper was killed with a twenty two. So was Abby. And the bullet in your mailbox was a twenty two. You and Abby were heard arguing a lot, too. She wanted to have a child and you didn't. Then she got pregnant and you couldn't have been the father. You killed Hopper because you thought he was. My guess is that you didn't know it was Bergman until Jane told you that Abby and Mort were getting it on. I know it all, Jane knows it all, or most of it, and the cops I told know it all, which is why they're on their way here.

You've had it, Jeff. What I'm not sure of is why you seduced Jane into all this. I could be wrong about that part, but I don't think so."

LaForge smiled. The Beretta was still pointed at me. My gun was in his other hand hanging down at his side.

"You know what, Ethan, I don't think you told anybody," he said quietly, as if he was thinking out loud. "You're too much of a hot dog for that. You'd want to get me by yourself."

His eyes narrowed and his face seemed to get harder.

"To answer your question, when Jane came to me about Mort and Abby I nailed her after about fifteen minutes. She was easy, kind of pathetic even, but it was like making love to a fucking stick. I'd decided right away that I might have a use for her. She doesn't know it yet, but she'll commit suicide. There'll be a note confessing that she killed Abby for seducing her husband, and killed Hopper before that because he was the third player in their little threesome. She actually *was* down here several times and I paid for the forged documents to make the timing look right. In Mexico, a little money in the right place and you can do anything. I did have to screw her a few more times to keep her going through all the booze. I'll take care of the suicide note, too. Mort will deny the threesome, of course, but who'll believe that stupid sap? I know now that Hopper and Abby never had anything going on, but I can't very well take it back, can I? It doesn't matter anyway. People love that kind of story, the more sordid the better. They'll believe it because they want to believe it. The whole thing'll ruin Bergman, of course. I'll kill his worthless ass later, in my own good time. I'm a patient man. So you see, Ethan, I'm still smarter than you. I always was. And now I'm going to kill you."

LaForge's hard look had passed. Now the smug bastard just seemed pleased with himself.

"How will you explain me?" I asked. "There are a lot of bodies piling up. You don't need one more."

"You do make it messy," he admitted.

And then he smiled.

"You know, this may be an opportunity. Maybe *you're* the one who threatened me? Maybe you had the hots for Abby, too, especially after your wife died. Maybe you always had it for Abby and carried a grudge against me for years? Everybody knows you don't like me. Yes, I like that. In death, you'll be just another pathetic jerk. I like it very much."

Jeff was wrong. He was anything but a patient man. That was his problem. His plan was too complicated, even preposterous, to work, but I had a more immediate concern; the gun pointed at my gut.

The Beretta was a semi-automatic. With a semi-automatic, you have to chamber a round for the first shot. According to Eckert, LaForge wasn't as expert as he thought he was. He was worked up, too. Did he remember? I'd have to rush him and hope. I didn't like my chances, but there wasn't any other choice.

Suddenly there was a crash at the front door and a male voice yelled something that I didn't catch. Jeff fired three quick shots. He remembered to chamber a round after all. I didn't look to see what or who he was shooting at, I just knew that he didn't hit anything with the third shot because I was on him and the shot went into the ceiling. I drove my shoulder into his midsection\ and we went over the back of a brown leather sofa. I rolled over Jeff onto the floor and got to my feet in one continuous motion. It took Jeff a fraction of a second longer to get up. He dropped my gun when I tackled him but he still had the Beretta in his other hand. I was on him again before he could get off another shot.

Instead of shooting, he hit me in the face with the Beretta. I felt the hard blow on my cheekbone but it wasn't enough to slow me down. Using both hands, I grabbed his wrist and twisted his arm behind his back. He got his feet on the sofa and pushed so that we fell over backward. I heard the Beretta fall and skitter across the tile floor.

As we scrambled to our feet again, I doubled LaForge over with a right to his belly. It was a good punch. I felt my hand go deep. Holding the hair on the back of his head with both hands, I brought my knee up hard against his face and he staggered backward. He tried to protect his face with his hands so I hit him in the belly again. When his hands came down I grabbed a fistful of his hair with my left hand and hit him in the face with my right. He sagged and I hit him again and again. He twisted his head from side to side, trying to escape. I pinned him against the fireplace with my body, put my left forearm across his chest and hit him again with my right. I was so focused it was like I was looking through a microscope. All I wanted to do was beat him to death.

Something tugged at my arms. I heard someone shout my name as I was pulled back and away from LaForge. My focus enlarged to take in the whole room. I was breathing hard. LaForge was curled into a fetal position on the floor in front of the fireplace.

I sagged toward the sofa, turning as I did. That was when I saw Garcia lying on his back just inside the shattered door. Valencia was down on one knee beside him talking into his cell phone.

I heard Valencia call for an ambulance.

I heard LaForge call weakly for help.

I saw Valencia stand, walked over to LaForge, and kick him. Twice.

And I heard him say, "Shut up you *cabron* or I'll kill you myself."

CHAPTER 42

"WHEN THE BOY got your message he called me. I told him to wait down the road until I arrived, but he went ahead on his own. He probably approached the house, looked a window, and saw what was happening. He burst through the front door like a young bull and it got him killed. He never even drew his weapon."

We were outside on my patio; just me and Valencia. The afternoon breeze had kicked up and the rustle of the palms should have been soothing. It wasn't.

"I missed the funeral," I said.

"I know. A broken cheek bone is a good excuse."

"That, and I hate funerals. I still should have been there. I liked him."

"I flew over and back on the same day," Valencia said, looking out at the horizon without seeing anything. "I spent every minute wishing that I was anywhere else, wishing that I could go back in time and change things so that it never happened. You didn't miss anything."

What I missed was Dina. I missed Brewster, too. I missed everything my life used to be. I felt even worse because at least I still had the life that Jimmy Hopper, Abby LaForge, and Ramon Garcia didn't.

"What happens now?" I asked.

"Everyone in your country and mine wants LaForge," Valencia explained. "Until the legalities of where he will be tried are sorted out, he will be kept in the federal prison in La Paz. The Bergman woman won't stop talking, even if it's through an alcoholic haze. Although she doesn't know everything that happened, she has confirmed much and seems pleased that so many people are paying attention to her. LaForge's team of expensive lawyers desperately wanted to make a deal, but that is just a reflex. Making deals is what lawyers do. They have nothing to work with."

"LaForge spilled it all to me anyway," I said. "But my testimony probably wouldn't be admissible even in Mexico because I engaged in illegal entry, though I don't guess it matters because you were able to put it all together anyway. No matter how you look at it, he's done. LaForge is going away, probably for the rest of his life. The only question is what country. He's too high profile to ever get parole, not with three murders.

"For once the celebrity he enjoyed so much will hurt him," Valencia agreed.

I touched my face. The swelling had gone down, but it was still tender.

"What about Hopper's wife and kids?"

"That is interesting. As I understand it, the new management at LaForge's corporation set up a trust fund to comfortably support her and her children for the rest of their lives, including college, if the children choose to go."

"There's a new management already? That was fast."

"You know the new one at the top," Valencia said. "She told us that you talked to her many times. Her name is Giordano."

"Linda Giordano? We'll I'll be damned." I shook my head. "You know, the thing is, I bet she'll be good at it."

There was one more loose end. My curiosity overcame my reluctance to bring it up.

"And what about Bergman?"

"There is nothing about him," Valencia said. "He was fired for being pain in the *cula*, but there are no charges against him in either country. Being stupid isn't a crime. We could put him away for hiring the men who attacked you, but unless you are eager to do that I don't think he's worth the trouble. He wouldn't last a week in one of our prisons."

"Yeah, let's just leave it," I said. "He'll probably get a job somewhere else. He's pretty good at what he did. He's just lousy at life."

We didn't say anything for a while. I still couldn't get my mind around it all. It would be a while before I could.

"You know, I wonder if Abby wanted to tell me a lot more than she did when I saw her at the house, but I cut her off," I said. "Maybe things would have been different if I'd let her talk. Garcia might still be alive. I'm so sorry. I liked that kid."

Valencia shook his head; measuring his own guilt and taking on mine at the same time.

"I was the one who got him involved," he said. "But he knew the risks. Young people always think they are invincible."

We sat there for a while and stewed in what might have been. The conversation was awkward, but we both felt that it was necessary.

"We were lucky to be dealing with an amateur," Valencia said.

"Yeah," I agreed. "The only thing Laforge did right was the initial misdirection, but that worked pretty well for a while. It fooled us all."

"His wife's body was his big mistake," Valencia said. "He didn't know what to do with it. Not many would. There was the gulf, but that required a boat and getting the body to a boat without being seen. He could have buried it, but where? Any serious digging increased the chance of exposure. There are other ways, but he either didn't know them couldn't figure out how."

I was glad that Valencia didn't go into detail about the "other ways" because I knew what most of them they were and they weren't something I wanted to think about just now.

"Jeff was the guy who always gave the orders for somebody else to carry out," I said. "He made deals, but didn't actually do anything himself. How do you dispose of a body? He didn't have a clue. Why would he? It's funny, but you could say that it was Abby who finally brought him down. Even in death, he didn't know what the hell to do with her."

CHAPTER 43

WHEN VALENCIA LEFT I called Linda Giordano.

"Congratulations," I said. "I just heard that you're the new CEO."

"Thanks, but I'm not quite there yet," she said. "How are you doing? I heard you got banged up.,"

"I'm OK. My head is nothing if not hard. What do you mean about not being there yet?"

"I have Mort's old job, at least for now" she explained. "The board figured that nobody knows the operation better than I do, especially once they heard my pitch. The board is leaving the CEO position open while it does some not very energetic head hunting. The unspoken agreement is that if I do well over the next six months, I get the top job."

"You won't do well," I said. "You'll do great."

"Thanks, Ethan," she said. "That's nice to hear. Things are a little overwhelming right now. I already made some moves to strengthen the company. We're selling Focus. It's too far away from our core business. Jeff just liked the high profile. Selling it will help pay down some of the debt we accumulated. Of the other acquisitions over the last few years, I'll keep some and sell some. What I can't sell and don't want to keep, I'll shut down. We need to run a lot leaner than we have. If I do it right, it won't be long before the bottom line will look a lot better that it has in a long while."

"That's great, Linda," I said, meaning every word. "Would you like to get together and have a drink to celebrate?"

"Believe me, I'd love to, but I can't right now," she replied. "What I need is for somebody to invent the thirty-hour day. Why don't I call you as soon as I get my head above water?"

"Sure," I said. "Anytime. Just let me know."

I had the feeling I'd been let down easy, but she promptly corrected me.

"I mean it, Ethan," she said. "I'd like that very much. I *will* call."

CHAPTER 44

I WASN'T awake and I wasn't asleep, but I knew I wasn't alone.

Dina was with me.

"How are you doing?" she asked.

"I'm okay, especially now that you're here."

"It was hard, though."

"Yes," I admitted, "it was hard."

"But you came out of it all right."

"You were there, kid," I said. "You always are."

"Ethan, we can't do this anymore. This is the last time."

I reached out in the darkness, hoping to find her.

"Don't say that. You can't go. You can't leave me."

"I love you but it's better this way. You've got to live your life and you can't do it if I'm always with you."

"But I don't want to get over you."

"That's why I can't come back. We love each other too much. You've got to go on. Just think of me sometimes and smile. You know, be sad, but not for too long."

And then she was gone.

A LOOK AT: CABO STORM
(CABO 4)

Private investigator mysteries don't usually come with movie stars, million-dollar egos, and hurricanes—but in Cabo San Lucas, chaos comes in waves.

When tabloid trainwreck and fading actress Rio LeDoux lands in Cabo to shoot a make-or-break blockbuster, she brings with her a storm of scandal, substance abuse, and bad decisions. Her slimy manager hires PI Ethan Cruickshank to keep her out of the headlines and out of trouble—a glorified babysitting gig Ethan only accepts because the money's good and the job seems simple.

It isn't.

As Rio spirals and tempers flare on set, one person goes missing. Then another. What started as a cushy gig turns into a full-blown investigation, one with shadows stretching far beyond the film set and secrets buried deeper than the beachfront villas.

Now, with a Category 5 hurricane bearing down on the Baja Peninsula, the bodies—and the stakes—are piling up fast. And in a town that thrives on illusion, Ethan must race to separate truth from fiction before everything is washed away.

Ethan Cruickshank may be battered, bruised, and barely hanging on—but he's the only thing standing between a killer and the perfect cover-up.

AVAILABLE SEPTEMBER 2025

ABOUT THE AUTHOR

Robert Wisehart was born in Indianapolis, Indiana, and now is fortunate enough to live in Santa Fe, New Mexico.

In between Indianapolis and Santa Fe, he worked for many years as an award-winning reporter and columnist for newspapers in Florida, North Carolina, Louisiana and Northern and Southern California, plus occasional flirtations with radio and television as an on-air commentator. Such is the changing world that three of the four newspapers no longer exist.

Later, as a freelance writer, Wisehart did everything from write speeches to ghost books. He labored as a restaurant critic and for a brief time as a one of the dreaded horde of government consultants, two words that can mean almost anything but usually add up to not much. His work has appeared in more than 200 newspapers and 30 magazines, plus several digital outlets.

Wisehart and his wife, Dana, have been married for a lifetime and intend to make it a very long lifetime indeed. They have moved much, traveled well and Dana easily is the best thing that ever happened to him. Their two sons, Marc and Carl, live in New York City.